Advanced Praise
for *The New Commandments*

"*The New Commandments* is a psychological thriller with a backdrop of international conflict, combined with spiritual wisdom, which will capture your imagination and may change how you view the world." **Elizabeth Carll, Ph.D., Psychologist, Author, Past President Media Division, American Psychological Association**

ॐ✝☾✡☆ॐ☾

"Brody has created a quick-paced tale that deals with religious issues while avoiding becoming too preachy in the process ... twists keep readers guessing to the end." **Kathe Tanner, *The Cambrian***

ॐ✝☾✡☆ॐ☾

"An exciting and refreshing antidote to the angry and judgmental challenges of these fear-based times, *The New Commandments* is both entertaining and hopeful–recognizing both the dangers and the spiritual possibilities of the human experience." **Reverend Ed Townley, Senior Minister, Unity in Chicago and Author of *Meditations on the Mount***

"Steve Brody's insight into the subject of conflict makes his work of fiction an interesting and important read." **Lois Capps, Member of Congress**

ॐ✝☪✡☮☉☾

"Steve Brody's *The New Commandments* offers a vision for peace in our modern world. The book is a meditation on the stresses and alienation of modern life, and on the pathways to a better life." **Bill Johnson, Author of *A Story is a Promise* and *The Combat Poets of Maya***

ॐ✝☪✡☮☉☾

"Weaving current events and universal tenets with sympathetic characters and artful storytelling, Steve Brody has created a spiritual page-turner. The message is clear. The time to embrace it is now." **Reverend Barbara Kowalska, B.A., B. Div., Interfaith Minister and Member of Many Voices of Faith**

THE NEW
COMMANDMENTS

Steve Brody, Ph.D.

CHAMPION PRESS LTD.

Milwaukee, Wisconsin

ALSO BY STEVE BRODY...

Renew Your Marriage at Midlife: a guide to growing together in love (co-authored with Cathy Brody, M.S.) Published by Putnam Publishing Group

CHAMPION PRESS, LTD.
FREDONIA, WISCONSIN

ISBN 1-891400-05-3
LCCN 2004105935

Manufactured in the United States of America 10 9 8 7 6 5 4 3 2 1

Dedication

"Blessed are the peacemakers:
for they shall be called the children of God."

Acknowledgments

There are some who believe enough in you as a writer to encourage you along the way. To Bill Johnson, Nina Catanese, Beth Skony and Jean Brody (no relation), thank you.

Then there are those who believe strongly in your work and join you along the journey. To my enthusiastic agent, Nancy Rosenfeld, and to my incredible publisher, Brook Noel, may the universe smile kindly on both of you for placing your faith in this book.

Greater still are those who teach you to believe in yourself, like my precious parents, who have supported me from day one. For that I have been truly blessed. And my children, who still believe in me as young adults: who woulda thunk it?

Special thanks to my spiritual family at the First Unity Church of Cambria for helping me know, truly know, that there is a Higher Self. Such belief is more precious than rain.

And finally, may I suggest that if you meet the Buddha on the road, marry her. I did, and now I believe in love. And that has been the greatest blessing of all.

Chapter One

Tuesday, May 11th—Los Angeles

DR. PETER HART HAD two cures for his loneliness and pain, both of which he practiced regularly: meditation and drinking. Evidence of the latter sat on his kitchen table when he stumbled downstairs to catch a late breakfast.

As he picked up the empty bottle of Jameson's and wobbled toward the garbage, his eyes were lured to a large bottle of aspirin. He wrestled with the top, managing a modest victory by opening it; small motor coordination wasn't his thing. In years past, he would have asked Marisa for help. She would have laughed, flipped the top off effortlessly, and then looked at him as if he was the most precious thing in the world. Placing three aspirin on his tongue, he swallowed the crumbling tablets in a gulp. A picture on the refrigerator caused his mind to drift back to Marisa.

Peter reached for the photo as if picking up a dandelion: like it might fall apart in his hand if he moved too quickly. Hadn't Marisa evaporated like that? Terra was only ten when the shot was taken—the three of them beaming from a sailboat off the coast of Mexico. How lucky she was to have had Marisa, Peter mused, especially with him gone so often. He sighed as he returned the photo to the refrigerator door. It was as if the past two years had been an endless low tide, and he, like some beached whale, was flopping and gaping about.

He fired up the coffee and cracked two eggs into a not-too-dirty bowl that had risen to the summit of the dishes in his sink. Beating the eggs with his right hand, he hit the power button on a small TV on the counter with his left.

A reporter's voice caught his attention. His right arm froze and hovered motionless over the eggs. His ears strained as if listening to the faint rumblings of an approaching storm. He knew White House correspondent Samantha Stone; she never lost control. She had been a reporter at the network for eighteen years, almost as long as he. Something wasn't right, he thought, as he turned up the volume on the breaking news story.

"Jonathan," she said in a high pitched voice to their anchor in New York, "it's highly unusual to see the president's staff this agitated."

Peter watched as Secret Service agents streaked across the White House lawn in the background. A lone bead of sweat pooled on Samantha's forehead.

Peter's hangover was routed by a rush of adrenaline. His stomach tightened. His mouth went dry.

"Sources close to the president have told us," his colleague continued, her eyes darting off camera to the right, "that the terrorist group responsible for last week's anthrax attack on Wall Street, the Islamic Party of God, was preparing an even more deadly attack here in Washington."

Peter noticed a second drop of perspiration above her upper lip as aides raced out the door in the growing chaos behind her. He gripped the small TV with both hands and lowered his head to within a foot of the screen.

"You can see the frantic pace of events here at the White House," she gestured over her right shoulder as a well-dressed man carrying a tall stack of papers tripped, spilling them on the lawn. Her head then jerked to the left while her body stiffened like a deer sensing danger.

Peter's screen went suddenly white before going black, but it was the initial blast of screechy static that disturbed him. The TV flickered back to life after a few seconds revealing the somber face of New York anchor Jonathan Hunter.

Peter watched him adjust his ear piece while producers off camera were presumably scrambling to understand what had happened. As the anchor filled the void with his usual singsong patter, he froze mid-sentence as if his brain had suddenly switched off. He then cleared his throat and looked straight to camera.

Peter knew that Jonathan's next few sentences would herald some inconceivable catastrophe. Something disastrous had just happened, and Peter's body tensed in anticipation.

"Ladies and gentlemen," said Jonathan, his voice shaking, "the White House has just been hit by an explosion, possibly a large bomb." He adjusted his ear piece again.

Peter's jaw dropped. He couldn't breathe. He watched as the anchor swallowed to regain his composure. "Ladies and gentlemen," he repeated, "what I'm about to tell you is, as yet, an unconfirmed report." He hesitated, but not in his usual rehearsed way. His eyes narrowed as he continued: "The entire capital has been rocked by the explosion. Again, this hasn't been confirmed, but it's being reported that it may have been a nuclear bomb."

Peter's lean body collapsed into an armchair by the television, his mouth open like a fish, his mind tumbling into a no-man's land of shock and disbelief. As a correspondent for the network, he had to get dressed and hustle to the station. He needed to move, but he wasn't sure how; it took him a while to stand.

He found himself upstairs in his bedroom and turned on the TV. Then he opened his closet and fingered some ties, but he couldn't see them through the tears. What about his cousin? His colleagues at APA? The tens of thousands of children? He picked up a shoe, but his body was too seized by a convulsion of grief to reach for the second one.

As if from another world, the news found its way back to him. Shoe in hand, he lurched toward the television. It was now being confirmed that a nuclear bomb had destroyed the capital. The White House, Congress, the Supreme Court, all gone. Hundreds of thousands of people dead. It would take a while to decipher how the bomb was delivered and by whom, most of the anchors agreed. But already the Islamic Party of God was claiming responsibility for the explosion.

"Maniacs, idiots," he shouted, as a wave of anger swept away sadness and fear. Those tides would return soon enough, he reflected. All the people, he kept thinking, all the people.

He knew he'd be called on to make sense of the madness, to walk viewers through the psychological aftershocks of disaster. He'd figure out something to say, to reassure them. But for the moment, he was as overwhelmed and confused as the next man. And every bit as devastated.

THE PHONE STARTLED him out of his stupor. "Peter, get your ass over to the news room," bellowed the familiar gravelly voice from New York. "The world's going to hell. You saw the news, didn't you?"

"Yeah, I saw it," Peter heard himself say as if from across the room. He knew he was experiencing some of the symptoms of acute stress. For him, and the rest of the country, he realized, everything would seem unreal or dreamlike, certainly for the next few days, and Peter was prone to feeling detached anyway. Even as a child, he had felt separated from the world—and love. Detached, never connected.

Joe Perelli was anything but detached. He thrived on trauma. "Peter, we need you live a.s.a.p.," he continued. "The whole fucking capital was blown away."

"I'm on my way, Joe," answered Peter, before closing his cell phone. The sudden quiet left him rudderless. He moved as if in deep water toward the closet. Rooting about for his other shoe, he noticed a sapphire blue tie Marisa had bought him in the British Virgin Islands. She had liked the way it brought out the color in his eyes. He folded it carefully and placed it in his briefcase along with his ear piece and make-up.

The memory of Marisa reminded him of Terra, not that he needed much reminding; she was his first thought when he had heard the news. But as a college junior in Santa Cruz, an hour south of San Francisco, she was in no immediate danger—even if the madmen had designs on other cities. But who knew anymore after 9/11?

Peter quickly dialed her, and she answered immediately. "Sweetie, is everything OK where you are?" he asked, trying not to sound worried.

"Yeah, I'm OK...." Terra's words slowed. "What's up?" Her voice was serious, sensing the heaviness in his.

"I'm on my way to the station, but I wanted to call and make sure you were all right." Then, more to himself than to her: "Thank God," he murmured.

"Why? What's happened?"

Peter didn't know what to say, and he hated to be the bearer of such news. "Washington was bombed, sweetie."

"Bombed?" her voice trembled. "What are you talking about?"

"The capital was destroyed," he whispered. Wasn't this the same soft, halting voice he had used when he told her about Marisa?

The line went silent. Peter suspected she was remembering that day, too.

"What do you mean, daddy?" she asked, sounding like an eight-year-old. "Destroyed how?"

"A nuclear bomb, sweetie." Again the slow whisper. "Turn on the news."

"I will, daddy," she responded. "Are you OK?" she asked, her voice edgy and frightened. "Where are you?"

"I'm at the house, here in L.A.," he reassured her. "I've got to get to the station. You know, to say something, try to help." He paused. "Will you be all right?"

"Yeah. Don't worry, dad. I've got my house mates."

He knew that she was trying to let him off the parental hook, and he was grateful for it. She had always been a trooper, especially when it came to his work.

"OK, sweetie. But promise to call me later, and let me know how you're doing."

"I will, daddy. Promise."

He paused. "I love you, sweetie."

"I know, dad." She sniffled, but didn't cry. "I love you, too."

Peter slowly folded the cell phone and slipped it into his pocket. More tears came as he shook his head in sad remembrance of when Terra was small and the world was full of Marisa's love and laughter. How he had taken those Camelot years for granted. An older colleague had warned him that he would never be as important as he was right then—to his adoring wife and young daughter. But he had raced off as a correspondent to pursue other fans and a spotlight he had lost in childhood, and now it was too late.

The leaves on the sycamore tree shimmered bright green as he spiraled down the outer stairs of his hilltop home. Yellow mustard and orange poppies shined in stark sacrilege to the somber mood of a world in mourning. Nature's gifts were oblivious to the breaking news of human stupidity. As far as Peter Hart was concerned, that's what this boiled down to—-stupidity. War and violence were a disgrace to the species, the ultimate failures—tragic and pathetic consequences of our lack of social intelligence.

He started the burgundy Volvo in the driveway and headed toward his home station, KNLA, ten minutes away. It was an unheard of commute for Southern California, but one Marisa had insisted on years earlier when Terra was little. It would give them more time together as a family, she had argued.

Three fully-armed security guards blocked the entrance to the station's parking lot off Sunset Boulevard. Generally a lone guard just waved Peter in, but today they examined his network ID and compared it to the downcast face in front of them. Only then did they open the gate.

The dust-covered Volvo floated into a parking space. Peter sat there for a moment, staring at a pile of pink apple blossoms that had fallen to the pavement. Hoping to break through the bastion of shock that had severed him from the world, he took one last, slow breath and shook himself into action. Another stern pair of eyes checked his ID as he walked into the building.

Clanking his way up the familiar brown metal steps, Peter tightened his face and entered the news room. It was typically a beehive of activity, and this morning it was swarming. A large black man with a bald head and a gold earring boomed, "Pete, over here." At six four and built like a bunker, cameraman Garrison "Bear" Edwards was a commanding presence. He waved Peter into an editing bay. "See that charred area on the left?" the big man pointed. "That's where the White House *was*," he explained, choking on the last word.

Peter put an arm around him. They had worked as a team for fifteen years and had witnessed many disasters, including 9/11, but nothing like this. The satellite pictures reminded Peter of photos he had seen of Hiroshima—a vast, flattened wasteland of rubble. Thousands of buildings, including the White House and the Capitol, either demolished or in flames. Landmarks like the Washington Monument non-existent.

"Here are the two questions Jonathan will ask you," interrupted his producer, Lucy Chang. A short woman in her mid thirties, she brushed back her dark hair as she popped her head into the glass booth. "I gave Perelli the usual ones about trauma and stress, if anything can be called usual," she added, looking away, fighting back the tears that seemed to be in everyone's eyes. "Most of today's focus is on the immediate impact of the disaster, so you've only got a minute. You're live in twenty."

She was about to return to her desk, when she paused and took a second look at Peter. "You OK, doc?"

Peter wasn't sure how to answer, because he wasn't sure if he was—everything was happening so fast. "Yeah, I'll be all right," he mumbled, sounding like he was at the bottom of a pool.

Lucy tilted her head to the side as if analyzing his response. "Doc, a lot of people need you right now,"

Peter nodded. He had felt the impact of the day's events, but only now did he remember his role as America's psychologist. He closed his eyes and took a deep breath. Perhaps his newfound ally, the silence, would cut through the numbness and guide him through the pain. He opened his eyes and repeated his earlier message, this time with conviction. "Yeah, I'll be all right," he smiled. "Thanks."

He turned and marched with renewed purpose toward his desk. He had been the network shrink for two decades.

Viewers relied on him to explain why they felt the way they did, and more importantly, how to cope with it. He scanned some copy, rolled up his sleeves and began typing.

"As you just heard from General Collier," continued Jonathan's talking head on a studio monitor near Peter, as the psychologist waited to go on the air in Los Angeles, "the president and most of Congress are believed to be dead as a result of the blast."

The anchor looked forlorn, observed Peter, as he watched him on the nearby screen. But the veteran journalist was also his best in a crisis, Peter concluded, for Jonathan had regained his composure soon after the story broke.

"Vice President Norton, we are now being told, is in a safe location and will address the nation shortly," the newsman continued.

"This has been a day unmatched in American history. The sheer magnitude of our loss has been overwhelming, as we grapple with shock, anger, sadness, and fear."

Peter knew they would soon toss to him in Los Angeles. He took a slow breath and steadied his glance at the camera some ten feet away. He then cleared his mind like the desktop of a computer and lowered the audio in his brain.

"To help us cope with this tragedy," continued Jonathan, "we turn to our psychologist correspondent, Dr. Peter Hart." Peter knew he was split-screen with the anchor now, but he wasn't nervous like in earlier years when ego and performance were center stage.

"Peter, take the pulse of the American psyche for a moment," asked Jonathan. "What are we likely to be experiencing, and how can we cope with this overwhelming catastrophe?"

Peter pictured a young mother he interviewed recently in Des Moines for a piece on postpartum depression and a salty truck driver he chatted with in Texas about retirement. He spoke to them as he answered, imagining their shock and sadness. It was an old broadcasting trick he had learned years ago, to personalize the cold and unfeeling camera lens.

"Jonathan, most of us are in a state of shock, disbelief and denial," he began. As he struggled to trust the silence above the cacophony of voices within his head, it rewarded his faith with a steady stream of words.

"This is just too horrendous and overwhelming to grasp," he continued. A satellite photo of D.C. flattened and in flames burned full-screen in his consciousness. "We're also likely to feel sad, terrified, and angry."

He imagined his Des Moines mom pausing to listen as she breast fed her baby, and the Texas trucker with grease on his hands watching from a stool in the garage.

He then ticked off more symptoms of acute stress, like numbness and detachment, and how some viewers might find it difficult to sleep or concentrate, while others might replay in their minds the same video clip of Hiroshima-like devastation which haunted Peter.

"So expect sadness and fear," he counseled. "It's normal to be upset during abnormal times." He was on a roll now, despite his own anguish—the consoling therapist reaching out to comfort a client.

"We'll need to pace ourselves during the days ahead. This may sound trite at a time like this, but don't forget the basics, like good sleep, proper diet, and exercise." Peter was a big believer in exercise and often walked in the hills by his home above Hollywood. "Talking things out with family and friends can also help."

Then, with an inner nod to the silence, he added, "And for those of you so inclined, double up on prayer and meditation. The research there is also quite positive." For Peter, he was beginning to believe it was a Godsend, literally. It had been his salvation since Marisa died.

A producer barked "30 seconds doc" into his ear while Jonathan asked the second question Lucy had e-mailed to New York: "What can parents do to help their children cope during this difficult time?"

Peter felt an immense sadness as he thought about the millions of kids who would be frightened by what they saw. "Listen to your children," he began, "and encourage them to share how they feel. It'll help."

This was a mantra he had chanted to parents since his first days in graduate school. In fact, he almost did his dissertation on four words: blocked feelings create distance. They certainly did in marriage, and most of that lesson, he believed, was learned during early childhood.

In Peter's case, it was the unspoken terror of sleeping alone in the basement after his sister had died. The black spider of his nightmares had been relentless. Peter had cried out, but no one had come, and eventually he stopped trying.

As a psychologist, he knew how people often distanced themselves from others, and their own emotional truth and well-being, because they hadn't felt safe in childhood. With that in mind, he added, "Reassure your kids about their safety and security, and avoid unnecessary separations if you can. They can make your child nervous.

"Finally, tell your children you love them." Like his conversation with Terra, millions of Americans, he imagined, would say something similar in the days to come, as this tidal wave of loss rippled across the country.

The network then switched from Peter full-screen to a shot of Jonathan looking at Peter on a large monitor in New York. "Dr. Peter Hart," replied Jonathan to Peter's image on the screen before him, "thank you, as always, for your insight and your counsel, especially during this difficult time."

"We're clear," whispered Lucy into Peter's ear piece. Bear shut down the lights, and Peter loosened his tie.

Lucy came out from the control booth and walked over to Peter. "Perelli wants you on set in New York tomorrow," she said.

"What about you and Bear?" Peter asked.

"He needs us to start on some packages for you. The usual victims and their families," she continued, staring vacantly at a row of monitors. "There's that stupid word 'usual' again," she added angrily. "We'll probably be in Baltimore, but the feds are telling Perelli that depends on the radiation plume." She paused. "The disaster center could be as far away as Philadelphia."

Peter shook his head. Bear sighed and mumbled, "Sweet Jesus."

Then, hesitating, Bear added, "Doc, while you were on the air, an estimate of casualties came in over the wire. A half million are presumed dead," he said, looking down at his shoes. "Several hundred thousand more are expected to die from the radiation."

Peter let out a whoosh. They had all lost colleagues in Washington. He put his arms around his companions and stood with them for a long time, a harbor of safety in a world of storm. Unaware of how much time had passed, he eventually broke anchor, gathered up his briefcase, laptop computer and make-up, and drifted down the hall.

He remembered the lyrics from an old folk song he played on the guitar in the '60s. "Where have all the flowers gone?" was hardly one of his favorites. Too syrupy. But its plaintive chorus, "When will we ever learn?" filled him with sadness and anger. Indeed, will we ever learn how to rein in the madness? he wondered darkly as the station door crashed shut behind him.

The upcoming journey was going to be a long one, he thought. And somewhere deep within he knew it would also change his life.

Chapter Two

Tuesday, May 11th—Washington, D.C.
American Psychological
Association Headquarters

PAM GORDON WAS locking her new Nissan Sentra in the underground parking garage after lunch before returning to her office on the sixth floor. She paused to admire the shiny aluminum-alloy wheels and glossy green paint job. At thirty-two, this was her first new car.

She loved being a public affairs officer with the American Psychological Association and lining up interviews for reporters like Peter. Seven months pregnant with her first child, breathing was difficult as she lumbered toward the elevator door. The stress from the anthrax assault on Wall Street five days earlier, coupled with threats of future attacks, also weighed heavily.

Despite the weariness, Pam grinned, patted her tummy and thought about her husband and soon-to-be family. Things were coming together nicely. They had even made an offer on a house in the country; it would be safer there to raise a family, they had decided.

The expectant mom was nearing the elevator when suddenly she was lifted and thrown the remaining ten feet. Her shoulder cracked as it crashed against the steel door. Then blackness.

Minutes passed, or was it hours? she wondered, regaining consciousness. Her bright green eyes searched the darkness. Black smoke was everywhere; its acrid taste threw her throat into spasm. The smell of gasoline from crushed cars permeated the air. The screams, however, were the worst part.

Barely breathing, she tried to stand, but couldn't. Her chest was pinned under a jungle of desks, plaster, and steel. It took a while to realize that the furniture was probably from one of the floors above.

Pam reached for a chair and used it as a lever to free her torso. The side of her face was bleeding, and her new maternity clothes were ripped and dirty.

Crouching to get below the smoke, she saw a man lying a few feet away—motionless and not breathing. She crawled toward him. Never having seen a dead person before, the shock weakened her arms and sickened her stomach. She vomited, mostly her lunch, but considerable blood as well.

Internal bleeding, Pam thought, still in a daze. This was not good; she had to get help, for herself and her baby.

Pam checked the man's body for a pulse; his torpid eyes stared at the twisted steel and concrete that was once a ceiling. She had seen him before, but they worked in different departments and had never met. Feeling no pulse, she closed his eyes and recited The Lord's Prayer.

Growing weaker by the moment, Pam collapsed from exhaustion halfway through praying. She cried faintly as she laid by the dead man's remains, picturing her husband and the baby she would never hold. Forty minutes later, shaking and cold, the young mother-to-be let out a final whimper, and died.

ALL TWELVE STORIES of Pam's building on the corner of First and G Streets had collapsed, as had the historic Union Station across the way. They were little less than a mile from the National Archives building on Pennsylvania Avenue, where the bomb had been detonated. That spot, analysts would later speculate, was probably chosen because it was directly between the White House and the Capitol, each approximately three quarters of a mile away. Both icons were mostly destroyed and now in flames.

ARLINGTON NATIONAL CEMETERY

GEORGIA PEMBERTON WAS laying white roses on the graves of the two men she had loved most deeply: her first husband William, who had died on the beaches of Normandy during World War II, and her only son Billy, who was killed by a sniper on this day in Vietnam forty years earlier.

At eighty-one, Georgia was still spry and independent. She had visited with William and was about to place flowers at the grave of the son he had never met. She adjusted her yellow sun hat while two blazing, red male cardinals whistled loudly as they contested for the attention of an unpretentious brown female.

Georgia was one of nearly four million people who visited the national cemetery each year. Despite such numbers, Arlington was quiet that day, befitting the somber nature of its mission and the thousands of young men who rested beneath the rows of graves that stretched over six hundred acres.

The sky was an immaculate blue, unblemished by clouds or the smog that occasionally wafted in from Washington. A lone jet rumbled overhead as it veered toward the west from Reagan National Airport. Lower to the ground, a mourning dove called from a nearby pine.

Suddenly a brilliant flash of bright light raced across the sky. Georgia blinked as it flew over the Potomac River and advanced toward her. An instant later, she was knocked off her feet, landing on grass.

She sat dazed as the day grew darker. Like most Americans of her generation, she had seen footage during the Cold War of atomic explosions. Her mouth dropped open as she watched what had once been only an image on a television screen become her reality.

Then she remembered her daughter and grandson. They had gone into the city to visit the Smithsonian Institute. She had asked them to leave her here for a few hours to be with William and Billy, the weather being mild on this May afternoon. She had lost her first husband, her son, and now she feared, her only daughter and grandchild.

They had, indeed, been vaporized by the blast, for they were only half a mile from the point of detonation. They were just about to enter the museum when the bomb went off. Two months from now a worker would notice the silhouette of a mother and child holding hands. It would be burned into the museum's outer wall. Georgia would never hear the news.

"Why them?" she cried out at God, more as an accusation than a question. First her husband, then her son, and now her daughter and grandson. All so young, and she so old.

Georgia didn't realize that soon she would join them, for she was less than three miles from the blast. The wind, though slight that day, was gently blowing a deadly plume of radiation her way. In two weeks her hair would fall out. Diarrhea and high fever would sweep through her body along with nausea and headaches. Her gums would bleed, and she would be unable to resist infection.

An entire family swept away by human conflict: Georgia's husband on the beach in Normandy, her son in Vietnam, and now the rest of the Pembertons, on a new battlefield of undetermined boundaries.

RUSSELL SENATE OFFICE BUILDING

SENATOR JOE FOWLER gazed from the office window where he had worked for the past twenty years. After three terms in the Senate and two in the House of Representatives, he still admired the stately grace of the Capitol dome across the street. At fifty-eight years old, he was preparing to run for president.

"We're with you, Joe. Just tell us when you need the money," said the pharmaceutical executive on the other end of the line. The senator smiled at the thought of five hundred thousand dollars as he ran his long thin fingers through a lean covering of grayish-brown hair. The early polls documented his lead. In Senator Fowler's mind, all that separated him from victory was money.

Jennifer, his trusted aide, breezed in and placed a memo in front of him. It was another warning about a possible assault on the capital. Joe dismissed it as an overreaction. There had been several such false alarms since the anthrax attack on Wall Street had killed three hundred people the week before. When he became president, he swore to himself, he would ensure that the country would be safe.

He crumpled up the note and hurled it toward a waste basket across the room. An All-American at Princeton, he could still shoot. He watched it sail by the window and then froze when he saw the sky light up around it.

In an instant shards of glass flew at great speed toward his face. Still in his chair, he was lifted and thrown across the room and then outside. Although he couldn't see it, the senator felt and heard fire all around him. He didn't know if it was from the blast or gas pipes that had ruptured. He didn't give it much thought. He was in too much pain.

The building had toppled, leaving the senator somehow alive in a heap a few yards from Constitution Avenue. He was still holding the phone, his mind struggling to understand how he had been transported outside from a second story office.

He tried to open his eyes and then realized that they weren't closed. He patted his torn shirt pocket for his glasses; it took a while to grasp that he was blind. *I can't die now*, he thought to himself. *Not when I have a shot at the presidency.*

An image of his beloved grandmother came to him and in a soothing voice told him not to worry. Everything would be all right, she reassured him. She began to sing an old Irish lullaby he remembered hearing during childhood.

"Tu-ra-lu-ra-lu-ra," she purred sweetly. The senator smiled as he felt her arms gently rock him. He died by the curb across from the Capitol near a pile of rubble that was once his office, the phone still in his left hand.

Chapter Three

Tuesday, May 11th—
Hollywood Hills, California

PETER DROVE THROUGH Hollywood on automatic pilot, his mind still a video rerun of D.C. desolate and smoking. He pulled over to dial his cousin, but all he heard was a continuous, frenzied series of sharp, high-pitched notes—like an out-of-control busy signal. It was the same maddening tone when he attempted to reach Pam Gordon at APA. He tried a few more friends in D.C., but with the same exasperating response.

The violence has got to end, he vowed, as he stopped for a brief walk in the hills before going home. *Why can't we just get along?*

He was sick of all the religious intolerance, which Peter blamed for much of the conflict. How ironic and tragic, he thought, that humankind's noblest desire to be with God should trigger so much hatred and destruction. Catholics fought Protestants, Hindus battled Muslims, and now this emerging "holy war" between militant Islam and the West—as if war could be holy.

He looked down at the city. Hundreds of thousands lived in the basin below: fathers on cell phones, babies learning how to walk, grandmothers knitting Christmas stockings. Washington, D.C., was like that. He choked up when he realized he was using the word *was*. He still couldn't believe it.

Sitting on a smooth waist-high boulder, he closed his eyes and began to meditate. *God, please help me, please help all of us,* he begged. His meditation was half prayer these days, as he often asked the silence for help. And God was no longer a word that didn't make sense, as it was during his early adulthood. Like many of his generation, he had rebelled against religion, and God. But gradually he had turned to meditation, and now even to prayer.

A warm light began to fill his consciousness, which was not unusual for Peter. He often experienced what he called the Presence or God this way. Sometimes the light was white; occasionally it was blue. But it always calmed him deeply.

With each breath, he instructed his muscles to loosen their grip and his mind to abandon all thought. It was a subtle letting go, but after years of practice, he had learned to descend into the stillness quickly. The light brightened and expanded, until it was all he could see and feel.

In the silence between thoughts, his consciousness extended beyond the confines of his head. It was an altered state, Peter acknowledged, but one he had grown to trust as perhaps no less real than ordinary reality. Each moment quivered with energy and rippled through time and space. He was a drop in the ocean of existence, but he was more the ocean than the drop.

Although he had undulated without boundaries in this sea of unity before, this time he heard something. It was a voice—a still small voice from within—but a distinct narration nonetheless.

"Bring them together," it said. "Pick up the torch. I will guide you." Peter startled and opened his eyes. He had seen images before and had revelations, but he had never heard voices.

I'm losing my mind, he worried, turning around to see if anyone had been watching. Another California psychologist hearing voices. Was he no different than the schizophrenics he worked with over the years? Wasn't one of the questions on a personality test he used, the MMPI, about hearing voices?

As if on cue, the piercing *kee-eee-arrr* of a red-tailed hawk ruptured the stillness. It was sitting on a utility pole nearby. It looked at Peter for a long time, jumped up and hovered above him. He gazed into its brown eyes as it screeched only ten feet overhead. Red-tails were not known to hover, so he was puzzled and frightened when the large raptor continued to flutter over him before disappearing to the east.

Peter went numb; the combination of the voice and the red-tail stunned and bewildered him. So Peter responded as he usually did when he was overwhelmed: he took one of his slow, deep breaths and closed his eyes.

The red-tail he could dismiss, perhaps, as an incredible coincidence. But a voice—from God? Peter didn't trust voices. They led to cockiness, and that often led to religious intolerance. How many well-intended zealots had killed in the name of the Absolute? he wondered.

A picture of himself stepping off a precipice formed in his mind, followed by the words "faith, not fear." Peter knew he was at a crossroads. Did he take the step or not? His body trembled and his stomach churned, but he had journeyed too far on the spiritual path to turn back now. Besides, what did he have to lose? what with Marisa gone. He took the leap of faith and waded into the stillness.

I will trust you as completely as I know how, he contracted with God, *as long as I feel love.* That would be the litmus test. If it was not love, it would not be God—at least not Peter's God.

The light within grew strong again and unwavering, but this time it encircled his heart. He had never felt such complete love, not even with Marisa. It was like being in the Garden of Eden. He smiled as he remembered another spring day half a century earlier when he played at his mother's feet while she trimmed red roses in a similar garden shortly before his baby sister died.

Enfolded within the light, he floated joyously, beyond need, beyond longing. There was no separation between him and the very ground of being, the implicate order, the Presence, the Great Mystery, the Light, God. So many words, thought Peter, for something so far beyond language.

"There are many expressions of faith," said the still small voice. This time he remained opened to God and did not doubt.

Peter's consciousness hovered as if in the middle of the universe, with billions of stars shining all around him. He had never experienced anything this intense or mystical, not even on psychedelics during his student days in the '60s.

"Help them to understand one another," God said. God was asking him, Peter Hart, to do something. His voice was gentle, but this was a commandment nonetheless; God doesn't do requests.

I will, answered Peter, from a still pool of quiet resolve. He wasn't sure how, but he trusted, as never before, that the path would unfold. It would be on God's time, not his. At a moment when the United States was immersed in possibly its worst turmoil ever, Peter felt a calmness, and completeness. How could he question this voice when everything felt so right? For the first time since Marisa's death, there was no fear, and no loneliness.

As he walked back to his car, he wondered what God had meant earlier about picking up the torch. "When it's time, I will guide you," reminded God, sounding like a patient parent with a six-year-old.

Peter smiled to himself and nodded slightly. Then he scanned the area again to see if anyone had been watching. No one was around: only the usual shrubs and rocks. Everything outside looked the same, but inside he felt profoundly different.

He started the engine and headed toward home. A million questions filled Peter's mind, but he also had found a powerful answer.

"YOUR FLIGHT LEAVES at three, Peter," said Lucy's voice on his answering machine. "We were lucky to find you a private plane out of Santa Monica; most of the airports are closed. Don't forget your new jacket," she added.

Peter did what he was told. He usually did with women, especially when they took care of him. That was part of the deal: he'd do what they asked, and they wouldn't leave him. It all went back to the nightmares, to being separated from his mom, and his fear of being alone. It was that same fear and loneliness that had driven him to drink after Marisa died.

Perhaps a quick shot of whiskey wouldn't hurt, he lied to himself, reaching into the cabinet. He cracked open a fresh bottle and rummaged through the freezer for ice; he loved the clinking sound it made as it hit the glass.

It was the queasy churning in his stomach that stopped him. He looked around the empty house and crumbled. Loud sobs shook his body like a hurricane buffets a small boat at sea. Thousands of babies, grandmothers, workers in the midst of their day, in the middle of their lives, crushed, burned, buried alive. The pain was staggering, nauseating. He hated himself for drinking at that moment, but he chugged it down nonetheless.

Guilty and uninhabited, he tramped upstairs to pack. He watched himself drag his new blazer from the closet. Sleepwalking through a nightmare, he gathered together the rest of his jackets, shirts and ties. He had been in the business long enough. He knew that when disaster struck, he might not make it home for weeks. Swallowing his pain, he headed out the door to help others with theirs.

The drive through town to the Santa Monica Municipal Airport threw him back into the world. Streets were empty. Drivers that hadn't reached home yet were teary-eyed or in a trance from shock; many talked on their cell phones. Everyone was listening to radio news updates, which were arriving in a frenzy from around the globe.

Peter again thought of his cousin in D.C. and colleagues at the American Psychological Association's headquarters there. Were they alive? he wondered. What about their children? Each face floated in with a wave of sadness.

He drove under the San Diego freeway as he neared the airport. Someone had hung a banner on the overpass saying "No Fear." It was a popular advertising slogan among young people, and he smiled at their courage and patriotism.

"No fear, Peter, that's the key," repeated the still small voice. It was the same voice he had heard earlier, the one they talk about in the Bible, he realized, but this time it didn't unnerve him. It was a half thought really, but it came from somewhere other than his usual self.

He wanted to have faith, especially now, but he was skeptical by nature, and by training: *Is this a deeper part of myself, or is this coming from some higher power?* He was leery of those who claimed divine intervention but didn't love, understand or respect anyone who believed differently. Wasn't it a similar, fanatical leap of faith that had emboldened these maniacs to kill hundreds of thousands of people?

Fear ran the show on a personal level, too, he realized. It was why he analyzed everything, and why love, peace and joy were often a thin veil away—although that veil had been a rope-thick web when he was a child. He shuddered remembering the nightmare. His parents, like the love and attention he had toiled for his entire life, were always on the other side of the web. The spider would snigger sinisterly, and they would give up and turn away.

"Faith, not fear," he said to himself, as traffic slowed for a red light. Maybe it would work: somehow muffle the cries of a world in pain and soothe the wounds of his broken heart.

He wanted to believe, to walk in faith, but he also knew that the journey was young, and he was only a toddler. He closed his eyes while waiting for the light to change and repeated his new mantra: "Faith, not fear."

EN ROUTE TO NEW YORK

PETER SLEPT UNEASILY while in his dream a young boy wandered aimlessly through the rubble that was once his neighborhood calling out "Mama, Mama." The five-year-old refused to believe that the charred remains lying outside his home were his mother, although he carried her severed arm with him as he walked.

He marched slowly toward Bear's camera and pressed his dirty face against the lens. "Where are you?" he asked sadly, as he looked into the camera for Peter. "Why won't you help us?"

That's when Peter realized, in his dream, that he was dreaming, and yelled "Cut." But behind the young boy, knights on horseback and Arabs on camels charged at one another with long swords instead.

As the crusaders neared the twenty yard line, the crowd stood up and sang "God Bless America." "Allah is Great," screamed the Arabs in their long white robes as they lined up their camels on the other side of the line.

A luminous falcon of light distracted the warriors and the spectators as it landed on Peter's shoulder mid-field.

"God told me to give this to you," said the falcon, handing him a pen with its talons. "It's mightier than the sword, you know."

Albert Einstein, one of Peter's heroes, walked onto the field and led the stadium in a chant of "write it, write it," as the words "World Day of Understanding" gushed like a fountain from Peter's pen. The crowd then linked arms and sang together in many voices of faith.

PETER AWOKE WITH a start between Los Angeles and New York. He pulled out his laptop, the chant "write it, write it" still echoing in his mind.

What am I supposed to write? he wondered, as he dropped into the silence.

"Just write it," said the now familiar voice. "Trust in me, remember? I will guide you."

Peter relaxed his body and allowed the Presence to pilot his fingers. He was awed at how easily they flew over the keyboard, and surprised, once he had finished, at the reasonableness of what he had written.

WORLD DAY OF UNDERSTANDING: MANY VOICES OF FAITH

Einstein warned that "The unleashed power of the atom has changed everything save our modes of thinking, and we thus drift toward unparalleled catastrophes."

We have witnessed one of those catastrophes today. If the attack on Washington teaches us anything, it's that we must end cultural misunderstanding and religious intolerance.

On Sunday, June 11th, to mark the one-month anniversary of the attack, many of us throughout the world will gather together in our own communities to listen to and learn about each other's spiritual paths and religious traditions.

Please join us on that day. Encourage your religious leader or local ministerial association to plan a meeting or service in your community to further the dialogue among our many voices of faith. And spread the word to others who also might be interested.

Together we CAN make a difference. Here's to greater understanding . . . a key steppingstone on the road to peace on earth.

Peace, Shalom, Salaam, Namaste . . .

Dr. Peter Hart

After Peter arrived at his hotel in New York, he e-mailed the message to everyone he knew, including religious leaders from around the world whom he had interviewed for a series on spirituality and health. After twenty years at the network, Peter had connections with many powerful people, from the Dalai Lama to the Senate Majority Leader. He also posted his message in a column he wrote for ThirdAge.com, and sent it to a distant cousin who had been a famous scientist in the former Soviet Union.

Although the morning news meeting at network headquarters was only hours away, he felt refreshed when he settled into bed. His last image was of the five-year-old from his dream smiling at him through Bear's camera.

Chapter Four

Wednesday, May 12th—New York

PERELLI CHEWED HIS cigar and paced back and forth like a caged tiger as Peter entered the network's national news room. "Half a million people were murdered yesterday," Perelli snarled at the assemblage of producers, assignment editors, and interns crammed into a conference room for the early morning briefing.

The balding executive producer for the nation's most watched evening news tried to hitch his wrinkled gray pants over his abundant belly, but with little success; cherry-colored suspenders kept them from slipping down entirely. "Some of these people were friends and family," he continued to roar. "The *least* we can do to honor their memories is help the country understand what happened, why, and how we can cope with it."

Peter ducked when he walked by the window, but Perelli saw him anyway and bellowed, "Peter, get your ass in here. We need some group therapy."

Peter loved his boss, and occasionally they drank a few beers together at Red's Place after the newscast. He called him Joe then, rather than Perelli. But the tragedy in Washington had softened Peter, and he smiled impishly as he responded.

"Joe, you're the kind of guy who redefines group therapy," Peter joked in a mock professorial tone. He paused to fuel the moment, as twenty heads turned in his direction. "You, and five therapists."

That got a chuckle from the room, as Perelli clutched his chest feigning a wounded heart. "Cute," he shot back. His face turned stormy, however, and Peter braced for lightning.

"Seriously, Peter, what's with this World Day of Understanding?" he asked, tossing a few sheets of paper on the desk.

Peter was shocked. How did Perelli get wind of it so soon?

"Cardinal O'Conner is holding a news conference about it with Rabbi Mandell, an Islamic mullah, and a couple of other swamis from religions I've barely heard of," shouted Perelli. He was all thunder now. "Jesus, Peter, we're supposed to report the news, not make it!

"It even hit the wire an hour ago," Perelli continued, now in a downpour. "Religious leaders in London, Paris,

Mexico City, and Tokyo are trying to reach you here at the network."

Peter was dumbfounded that his call for a World Day of Understanding would have such impact, and in so short a time. But he was also embarrassed. It was a basic tenet of journalism not to let one's personal or political leanings interfere with reporting. Perelli was right to be angry. Peter had become so swept up by events that he completely lost his perspective. How could he be so blind?

Perelli ended the meeting, motioned Peter into his office, and closed the door. "Duncan will probably have your ass for this," he warned. He rotated his round body toward the window and gazed across the city, squinting his tired eyes.

Peter lowered his head in obeisance like a kid in the principal's office.

"Look," continued his boss, his voice softer, "none of us is in his right mind right now." He paused. Then, shaking his head and turning back toward Peter, he whispered, "those bastards." He stared at a picture of his grandchildren. His eyes grew waxy, his gaze inward. Again, the whisper: "It could have been New York, you know."

Peter sighed. "I know, Joe."

They stood in silence, like old friends at a funeral.

"Take the rest of the day off and do some damage control," said Perelli, returning to his desk. "I'll try to cover for you."

Peter looked at his boss like a wounded dog looks at his master. He was grateful for both the protection and the friendship Perelli had extended. "Thanks boss," he said. "I won't let you down." He gave him a nod, clamped his lips together, and walked out the door.

IT WAS NINE O'CLOCK. Peter decided to walk the eight blocks or so back to his hotel room off Columbus Circle near Central Park. It would give him time to clear his head.

The city was quiet. No horns honked. No one ran or yelled for a cab. Those that had come to work looked dazed, drifting like phantoms, their minds on pause and far away.

Peter watched a refrigeration serviceman descend into a cellar nearby, much as his father had done here a generation earlier. He remembered holding the flashlight for his dad during similar calls in dark, rat infested cellars, especially after his sister died and his mom was driven away to a hospital in the mountains for her depression.

Spiders hadn't scared him in those basements, as long as his dad was with him. His father would tell him stories about the places he had been in Europe and Africa during the great war, and how important it was to do your part when the world needed you.

Peter had tried to honor that calling, to do his part. It was at the heart of his efforts to bridge differences between people, as a journalist as well as a psychologist.

He looked up at the skyscrapers and tried to imagine the horror of what happened in Washington. Could he do anything about the madness? he wondered. He doubted it, but he knew he had to try.

His mind tightened in turmoil as he entered his hotel room. What was he to do about this World Day of Understanding? Given what Perelli had told him, could he do anything about it now anyway?

Peter collapsed into a chair and opened his laptop. Lost in thought, he plugged it in and hit the receive button. The name Unity Mexico appeared on his incoming messages. Then Methodists International, Prime Minister Kingsmill, The Dalai Lama, Shii Islam, Gandhi.edu, National Council of Churches, Bette Midler, Episcopal USA, Krishna.org, European Jewish Congress, The Carter Center, and The Vatican, until his inbox filled with responses to his World Day of Understanding— eighty-six in all!

Peter leaned forward, scrolling up and down the long list, his breath caught in his throat. The first one was from the president of the Unity churches in Mexico promising to organize all of Central and South America.

> Dear Peter,
> Hace mucho tiempo since we talk on the Spanish feed (si esta correcto?), but nosotros aqui in Latin America are many and strong for peace.
> Our hearts and prayers are with you in Los Estados Unidos. It is so sad, this world.

I have e-mailed the other Unity churches in the Americas, and know that we are one peoples for your World Day of Understanding.

Muchas, muchas gracias senor Peter! Su dia es muy importante!

Tu amiga en Paz,

Terecita

Peter closed his eyes and slowly exhaled. Laughing and crying at the same time, he read how other churches pledged to do the same in Europe, Asia, and Australia. There were messages of support from Islamic mullahs in Iran and Indonesia, Hindu and Jewish leaders—even politicians and movie stars.

"Maybe we *can* change our modes of thinking," read one from the Senate Majority Leader. "Clearly we must try. My office can petition those of us left in Congress to declare the Sunday of June 11th a National Day of Understanding. Are you interested?"

Maybe we can indeed, Peter murmured, reading Senator Matthews' e-mail a second time. But Peter was also anxious; could he shoulder such a load? he worried.

He closed his eyes and invited in the silence, picturing the five-year-old from his dream. *Please, God, grant me the strength, the love and the light,* he prayed quietly, *that I may do my part, to help bring peace to our troubled planet.*

As the light within him grew brighter, his computer chimed, signaling the arrival of another e-mail. He thanked the Presence, opened his eyes and read the message.

Dear Peter,

Forgive me for writing you at such a terrible time. You may not remember me. It was many years ago. You were a student of mine when I was a young poet in residence at Reed College in 1968.

Maybe you remember the Sufi poet we studied back then? Your favorite Rumi poem was "A perfect falcon, for no reason, has landed on your shoulder, and become yours."

Perhaps this World Day of Understanding has landed on your shoulder and become yours? God knows, Peter, we need something like this!

At any rate, I have followed your journalism career, and I suspect you're in New York by now. I am visiting from Cairo and am staying near Lincoln Center. I'd love to see you, or help in any way I can.

In Love & Light,
Rabia

Peter's body froze. He couldn't swallow. Hadn't he just asked for love and light? And the perfect falcon. *It landed on my shoulder,* he mumbled in disbelief, remembering the dream. *It even gave me the pen to write "World Day of Understanding."*

He had to see Rabia, and banged out a quick reply, inviting her to lunch at an Afghan restaurant across the street from Lincoln Center. Rumi would like that, he chuckled, remembering that the 13th century poet had been born in Afghanistan, then a part of the Persian empire.

He clicked send, and a few minutes later, she responded yes. *She's only a few years older than me,* he thought to himself, barely containing his excitement. He had forgotten the crush he had on her in college.

ALTHOUGH PETER HAD continued to read Rabia's poetry after graduating from Reed, it was the Rumi poem about the falcon that blazed in his mind as he opened the door to the restaurant and stepped inside.

He looked around and saw an attractive woman in the back, but dismissed her as too young. *Rabia must be at least sixty,* Peter said to himself, as he surveyed the room for older women. Not seeing any, he chose a seat by the window and waited. He was puzzled when the good-looking lady in the rear got up from her table and walked over to his.

"Peter Hart," she smiled, "I'm your old teacher, Rabia."

"Old teacher, indeed," he joked, as he shook her hand. "You look marvelous." His eyes scanned the tall, striking woman with long black hair, peppered with streaks of gray. A crimson rose glowed from its perch over her right ear. While her turquoise top was pleasantly low cut, it was the brilliance of her smile that most attracted him. He hadn't seen such radiance in a woman since his wife Marisa passed away.

Peter was so mesmerized that he forgot he was still holding Rabia's hand. "Oh, I'm sorry," he mumbled, sounding like a school boy. "Please sit down." He lowered his gaze to the floor, but his embarrassment turned to desire when she took the seat opposite his and crossed her long, athletic legs.

"This idea of bridging differences between peoples," she said, her accent a melodious mixture of French, English, and Arabic. "We must make it as important as air, Peter, for we will not survive without it."

He had forgotten how beautiful her voice was. As her student, he had loved listening to her read Rumi aloud.

"It has been a fire for me," she continued, "ever since our family was forced from Palestine. My father died a broken shopkeeper in Jerusalem. We *must* bridge these differences, Peter." Her large eyes gleamed like twin stars in a dark sky, as her body leaned toward his.

Peter looked away, feeling guilty for being aroused by her beauty, especially in light of what happened in Washington. But it was beauty, he recalled, that was at the heart of her passion. During adolescence she had re-named herself Rabia, she had told her students, after the great female mystic who wrote poetry in Persia during the eighth century. The original Rabia believed that God should not be loved out of fear or hope, but for his beauty, which resides in the heart. That message was at the core of the modern day Rabia, Peter realized.

He had read the fervid poems that had won her the Nobel prize in literature, and her syndicated column was a rare and powerful voice in the Arab world for peace and reconciliation. She had wrestled with her anger about the Israeli occupation and had not succumbed to bitterness and violence.

"The many voices of faith you wrote about, Peter," Rabia continued. "Rumi says, 'There are hundreds of ways to kneel and kiss the ground.'" She put her fingers to her lips, then gently lowered her hands to the table—but to Peter they looked like undulating cobras.

She paused, and they just looked at each other for a long moment. Peter broke the silence. "You speak as beautifully as I remember," he said, still in a trance. "I would love to have your help."

Then, blinking himself back into the room, he looked at her with a sense of urgency. "In fact, I need your help," he continued. "This World Day of Understanding has taken off like a rocket, and I have no idea where it's going."

She placed a hand over one of his. "Then we will ride it together," she reassured him, as a mother might comfort a child. Their fingers lingered together on the table, until Rabia's face turned red, matching the flower over her ear.

"I'm sorry," she apologized, pulling back her arm. "I shouldn't have jumped in so quickly. I'm not thinking clearly. I keep picturing all the people, especially the little ones . . . ." She looked away, her large eyes overcome with tears.

"I understand, truly," said Peter, sensing it was his turn to reassure her. "I felt less alone when you touched my hand, though. And like I said, I need help." She looked away, but Peter leaned his head to the side and insisted on eye contact. "We *all* need each other at this point," he argued.

"Thanks," Rabia said, drying her tears. "I needed that. The crying, that is," she smiled. "Well then, what is to be done?"

Peter updated her over lunch about the e-mails he had received.

"I have a thought," Rabia jumped in, swallowing quickly and grabbing her cell phone. "What if I call my friend Susan Crane? She heads the Unity church in Manhattan. We were close when I lectured here at Columbia. I think she'll let us use her phones and fax lines, and we can set up shop there."

"Great idea," Peter responded, but inside he was hesitant, remembering Perelli's warning.

Rabia punched in the church's number. She and the minister shared their shock and grief over Washington. Rabia then motioned for Peter to lean in when she asked Susan about using her church.

"Rabia, this is unbelievable," said the minister. Peter could hear her excitement. "National called only twenty minutes ago. Our entire church is being mobilized to support this World Day of Understanding."

"Not only that," she continued, "but Cardinal O'Conner along with a rabbi and the mullah from your old mosque asked me to join them and a few others to spearhead things in New York. We're holding a news conference at three."

Rabia flashed Peter a look of excitement. He appreciated her enthusiasm. This was indeed taking off like a rocket, and now Rabia knew it. Perhaps she also realized why he felt so overwhelmed.

"Can Dr. Hart join us at the press conference?" asked Susan. "It would be an honor to have him lead us. After all, this is his idea."

Rabia looked at Peter. They told Susan they'd think about it and call her right back. It was almost two.

"Whoosh," exhaled Peter. "This is a big one." He fiddled with the check. "Like my boss said, we're supposed to report the news, not create it."

"I know," agreed Rabia. "It's one thing for me to be opinionated; I'm a columnist. But you . . . . " Her voice trailed off as their waitress picked up the check.

"Yeah." He looked out the window and then back at Rabia. They both knew the rules. Peter was a correspondent; he was supposed to be unbiased and apolitical.

"On the other hand," he brightened, "if I've learned anything over the years, it's that you've got to honor your passion and the uniqueness of your own journey. Give me a minute, would you?"

He walked outside, leaned against the warm brick wall of the restaurant, and closed his eyes. The street was quiet. Only the most unruffled of New Yorkers were at work today, for it was still only twenty-four hours after the attack. It didn't take him long to connect with the silence.

"Faith, not fear," said the still small voice. Peter listened, but heard nothing more.

Then, from a distance, a flapping of wings announced the arrival of a large white falcon. Its downy pinions were like those he had seen in paintings of angels. "You must do your part, Peter," said the angelic bird from the north, its body now full-screen in the theater of his mind.

Peter watched as an image of himself approached the feathery wings and became enfolded by them. The figure then emerged from their embrace with white-tipped wings of his own. Peter had become an arctic falcon, and it was his job to circle the boundaries of the earth.

He opened his eyes and re-entered the restaurant. His mission was clear. "I can't ignore a perfect falcon," he said to Rabia. "Tell Susan we'll be there."

ELBURZ MOUNTAINS, IRAN

VLADIMIR SOROTNIK, PETER'S distant cousin, stared out the small window of his guarded room and prayed, although he didn't believe in God. He was a scientist, and the universe danced to laws of creation, not a creator.

He watched the moon dart in and out of an abundant bevy of ashen clouds as they flew in from the Caspian Sea. He had pieced together from his captors that he was near the coastal town of Tankabon in northern Iran. The capital, Tehran, was on the other side of the mountains, he had figured, further away to the south.

Vladimir glanced nervously at the door in case the guard, or worse, Ashraf himself, was to check on him, but he didn't expect either—just yet. He extracted a rusty screwdriver from under a loose floorboard. He was making progress, he smiled, as he worked to free himself from the lock that chained him to his bed at night.

Pulling a handkerchief out of the vest pocket of his tweed jacket as it lay draped over a chair by the dresser, those being the only pieces of furniture in his sparse room other than the bed, he wiped the sweat off the front of his balding head. Then he set down his wire-rimmed glasses; it would be easier to press the side of his face against the door without them.

He was a product of the old school, he recognized, folding the hanky and returning it to his pocket, when handkerchiefs and respect for authority still mattered, although he didn't miss the KGB. The new Russia was chaotic, but at least he wasn't besieged by bureaucrats and spied on by agents.

As one of the former Soviet Union's premier nuclear scientists, he had led the good life. Retirement hadn't been as sweet, but his life in Moscow had been pleasant, almost boring, he reflected—until two weeks ago.

THE SOROTNIK FAMILY had been on vacation at a seaside resort near Fort Shevchenko in Kazakstan, about five hundred miles north of Iran, when three men stormed the front door during dinner, gagged and blindfolded Vladimir, his wife and young son, and dragged them away to the deserted farmhouse that was now their prison. They had bounced in the back of a small hidden compartment of an old truck for many hours to get there, much of it on bumpy, dirt roads.

Ashraf, the notorious leader of the Islamic Party of God, greeted them when they arrived. A dark man with an even darker vision, he wore a deep scar on his right cheek and a black patch over his left eye—just as Vladimir and the rest of the world had seen on TV.

He terrorized them right from the start, slapping Vladimir's wife, Katerina, in front of the anxious husband and their six-year-old son; little Ivan wet his pants and howled liked a frightened animal.

Ashraf's men then chained Katerina and Ivan, spread-eagle, on the white stucco wall in the dining room, while Ashraf, in a cold but matter-of-fact voice, informed Vladimir that if he did not teach his scientist, Saeb, how to arm and deploy a nuclear device, Vladimir and his family would be killed—slowly. The Russian scientist didn't think that the Islamic Party of God had a nuclear weapon, but he might have helped them anyway after hearing little Ivan scream.

He had cooperated for two weeks, drawing detailed diagrams and teaching Saeb everything he could, until yesterday, when another mysterious crate arrived. Vladimir, deciding to investigate, had climbed out a bathroom window, while his guard waited outside; he then tiptoed into the barn to check it out.

After lifting the matted burlap covering, he had gasped loudly, startling Ashraf's black stallion and almost waking the guard dozing in the loft. But he could not dismiss what he had seen: there, on the crate, were the familiar markings of a Soviet-era nuclear device.

As he hustled back through the bathroom window to cover his tracks, he had wondered whether three other crates that had come and gone when he first arrived might also contain nuclear weapons. Could this be why his captors frequently referred to four cities: Washington, Tel Aviv, New York, and London?

His mind had flinched at the possibilities. It was then that he made the painful decision to escape that night and alert the world, even at the risk of his family.

A SLIVER OF moonlight beamed through the barred window as Vladimir finished wrestling with the lock. He then got back in bed. The guards checked every three hours, so he would bide his time until after the next inspection. He didn't have long to wait; they had come by at nine, and it was now almost midnight.

Vladimir heard the bolt crack open and watched from under the corner of his blanket as a burly guard in his early twenties rotated the door slowly on its hinges. The man stood back from the door, Uzi at the ready, just in case Vladimir had any ideas of escape. After reassuring himself that his prisoner was still asleep, he closed the door and returned to his post in the hall.

Vladimir waited a few minutes before slipping off the manacle that chained him to the bed. He tiptoed to the door, put his ear to the splintered wood, and smiled. The guard had stayed true to form and was snoring loudly enough for the scientist to detect. The timbre and pitch of the man's snorting and wheezing sounded better to Vladimir than any Bach concerto he and Katerina had ever listened to in Moscow.

He tapped a signal to his wife on the opposite wall. It was risky business, but the lone female guard, Leila, who usually stood watch outside Katerina's room, wasn't as strict about such matters, often giving little Ivan extra bread and water, and occasionally allowing the three of them brief family visits. Katerina knew about her husband's plan, and approved. When she tapped back to say good-bye, he wondered whether he would ever see her and their six-year-old again.

Vladimir swallowed hard, and went into action. He had been a swimmer in his youth and was still in excellent shape. He grabbed the sheet off the bed for later and pushed the dresser into the center of the room. Then, placing the chair on top, he hoisted himself through the narrow skylight, praying, in his agnostic fashion, that he didn't disturb the guard outside.

He wrapped the bed sheet around the brick chimney, shimmied down and slipped into the night. He had three hours, he calculated, before they would notice he was gone.

Chapter Five

Wednesday, May 12th—New York

THE STREET WAS still empty and quiet when Peter left the restaurant with Rabia. It took a moment to find a cab. They then headed crosstown to the United Nations building.

He didn't have to tell the cabby to put on the news; it was everywhere. Of the half million who had died, experts estimated that at least 150,000 had burned to death, some in temperatures measuring thousands of degrees. The remainder died from other injuries, like falling debris from collapsing buildings.

Arriving half an hour before the press conference, Rabia introduced Peter to Susan Crane. Network affiliates and independents were already scrapping for camera and mic positions, although given the enormity of the disaster in Washington, they seemed more subdued and cooperative. That didn't stop them from feeling scooped, Peter surmised, when he met with presenters in a pre-conference huddle off to the side.

An old man in a rich red robe shuffled toward him. "Dr. Hart," said Cardinal O'Conner, shaking his hand solemnly, "these are terrible times." He was stooped with age, but his eyes were like lasers as they looked deeply into Peter's. "We need your World Day of Understanding," the cardinal continued, "and we need you to lead it. It can't come from one of us," he explained, pointing to a dozen or so spiritual leaders who had joined him to address the press. "It must come from someone on the outside." The group nodded in agreement.

Besides the cardinal and the Unity minister, Rabbi Mandell and the Islamic mullah were there too, just as Perelli had scolded him about earlier that morning. Peter knew he'd have to come clean with his boss after the news conference, and he winced at the thought. But like his mother-in-law used to say, "Worry about things in order of their appearance." It was good psychology, he often lectured, as well as common sense.

Returning to the moment, he noticed Hindu and Buddhist leaders also present, along with other faiths. They were pleased when Peter asked them to join hands in a brief prayer circle before facing the press.

He did it for spiritual reasons, to honor the suffering of those in Washington and to bring the group together, but his media savvy subconscious also knew that intriguing video was the red meat of television news. An image of the world's religions holding hands and praying together was exactly what Peter wanted to feed these lions. He knew how the photographers would appreciate the scraps; it would give their editors and producers something other than talking heads to work with that evening.

"Let us pray," began Peter, as the spiritual leaders closed their eyes and bowed their heads. "Dear God of many names, please be with us as we join hands and seek your counsel, your wisdom, and your love."

The crews were upon them now, shooting from a variety of angles, but the prayer circle held fast. Such people were not easily disturbed. Their faith was their rock and fulcrum; all else was window dressing.

"Please be with those who suffer in Washington, D.C.," Peter continued. "May your love and peace heal their bodies and comfort their spirits. And may you bring solace to their friends and family, especially the children."

Rabia watched from the side. Her head was bowed, the pavement below her moist with tears.

Losing himself in the light, Peter arched his neck back, and with eyes still closed, pleaded toward the heavens. "Help us, O Great One," he begged, his voice breaking, "to understand one another and to be more tolerant of our differences. Although we speak to you in many voices, we are all your children. Teach us to walk together in love."

Mullah Kolkailah chanted the Al-Fatiha, the opening Sura read by Muslims before any reading from the Koran proper. His high, nasally voice echoed off the buildings, further deepening Peter's awareness of the Presence. Rabbi Mandell rocked back and forth as he pleaded in Hebrew that the Lord God was One. A Buddhist monk tapped a resonating prayer bell, each ring rippling through the crowd like a gentle breeze on a lake. And a Baptist minister recited a passage from the Sermon on the Mount: "Blessed are the peacemakers," preached Jesus, "for they shall be called the children of God."

After each of the religious leaders shared briefly in the prayer circle, they also took turns at the microphones addressing the media. Most of the attention focused on Peter, however, as the project's originator.

"Dr. Hart," challenged a zealous, baby-faced competitor from another network, his flaxen blond hair neatly in place. "What do you say to those who might perceive your movement as unpatriotic?"

Peter was used to firing off questions, not fielding them, and for a moment he wondered why he had accepted this mission. Was he up to the task? he worried. And was he doing it for the right reasons? He didn't trust his unconscious need for attention; it had seduced him many times in the past. Was this calling another veiled ego-fest, another truck load of recognition to fill the unseen emptiness and help him feel important?

He closed his eyes and took a deep breath. "Faith, not fear," his inner voice reminded him. It hadn't answered all his questions, but it helped center him as he stepped toward the microphones.

The reporter cocked his head to the side like a fox sizing up a rabbit. "Are you suggesting there's no evil here?" he contested. "Are we not to track down and hold responsible those who committed this heinous act?"

Peter studied the reporter. "Your point's well taken, Alan," he replied. He meant it, too, which surprised him. Not long ago he would have suited up for conflict and battled for pride. Spirit, however, demanded better. It was time to be open, to risk genuine dialogue, to pursue deeper and more mutual understanding.

It made him nervous to be this vulnerable, but he was tired of fighting fire with fire, anger with anger. Life had been one long chess game, and Peter was tired of playing games. *Win less, help more*, he said to himself. Underneath this reporter's attack was also a need for justice. If Peter was espousing that we understand and respect one another's differences, he had to model it himself, here and now.

"Certainly violence must be stopped and the perpetrators brought to justice," he acknowledged. "But we must be careful not to demonize other cultures along the way."

Peter had seen many spouses in therapy typecast a partner as the problem rather than work cooperatively to resolve their differences. It was seldom a matter of good versus evil, right against wrong. Usually each side had some version of truth and light. Harmony came when partners were able to hear the legitimate concerns underlying one another's positions.

"If history teaches us anything," Peter continued, "it's that we don't learn much from history. For countless generations we have picked up stones, swords, and eventually guns to resolve our religious and cultural differences, only now the weapons are truly catastrophic."

He wasn't sure if it was ego or Spirit, but he was on a roll now. He looked over at the sidelines and caught Rabia smiling at him.

"As Einstein warned," Peter concluded, "'the unleashed power of the atom has changed everything save our modes of thinking, and we thus drift toward unparalleled catastrophes.' Today we commit ourselves to changing those ways of thinking." He thanked the press and waved off further questions.

Before the religious leaders disbanded, they agreed to provide Peter with logistical and financial support. They also pledged to encourage their colleagues in other parts of the world to reach out to the different religions in their communities.

Each locale would plan its own event for Sunday, June 11th, and the entire world would pause for a Day of Understanding. All over the globe different faiths would commemorate the one-month anniversary of the attack on Washington by listening to and learning about each other's spiritual paths and religious traditions. A new movement was gathering steam, and Peter was the lead engine.

Heppner, Oregon

VERN BRENNAN, AN angry barrel of a man, sprang from his scruffy recliner when he saw Peter on CNN. "That son-of-a-bitch," he yelled, tossing a mostly empty Coor's can in the direction of his run-down TV. "Who the hell does he think he is!"

The pastor of a small group of militant fundamentalists, Vern collected guns and taught a handful of followers survival techniques on his farm along Willow Creek in the Blue Mountains of Oregon. They were proud to be among the 75,000 extremists collectively known as Christian Identity, most of whom lived in the Northwest.

The Last Days of the Bible would not be a time of rapture for Pastor Vern. They would be a pitched battle against the forces of evil during the Biblical interval of Tribulation, and that train was fast approaching. Vern could hear its whistle growing louder, especially after Satan unleashed his fury on the capital.

"Aurelia," he bellowed, storming into the kitchen. She was startled, her body expecting another blow. She hated it when he drank, especially lately. In her bones she knew Vern was going over the edge, but her capacity for love and loyalty knew no limits. Her denial was reinforced by her fundamentalist belief in self-sacrifice, which for Aurelia had carried her over the thin line separating religious orthodoxy from psychological pathology.

She looked up from fixing supper and smiled demurely, feeling strangely safer with a large cutting knife in her hand. "Honey, now don't get yourself all worked up over that stupid psychologist. He's not worth it."

Vern considered her advice for a moment, but it was short lived, as his mind jumped like a steel magnet back to Biblical verse. "This man is the Antichrist!" he shouted, his face reddening, the veins in his thick neck bulging. "Preaching peace before the Messiah's return is heresy, Aurelia—especially after Washington. It defiles the word of God."

Aurelia stepped toward him hesitantly. "Here, honey, I made your favorite," she said softly, trying to soothe him with a large steak like a zoo keeper with an angry lion. She gambled, touching him on the shoulder, hoping he'd let her massage his back. It worked, this time, although the time before she hadn't been as fortunate.

"That bleeding-heart bastard," Vern continued to rave, his teeth ripping into the blood-red meat as Aurelia massaged the twisted muscles in the back of his neck. "Armageddon is around the corner, and he thinks it's time for Sesame Street." He suddenly grew quiet, which scared Aurelia even more. That was when he was most dangerous.

"Pack my bags, Aurelia," he said softly, as if in a dream. "I'll be gone for a while." He chewed slowly, staring at the dark mountains through the kitchen window. "I've got God's work to do," he added, as he drifted out of the room.

It was Aurelia's turn to stare vacantly out the window now. The last time he was like this, an abortion doctor was murdered in Portland. Vern had returned soon after, and

Aurelia had seen him bury a rifle and scope in the woods behind their barn.

"Honey, please don't go," she finally replied, her mind racing as she searched for something to divert his attention. "At any rate, not just yet," she cooed, untying her apron as she followed him up the stairs to their bedroom. Beef would be the entree, she smiled to herself; she would be the dessert.

She grabbed a little-used bottle of French perfume from the back of the medicine cabinet as she passed the bathroom. Pulling down the high collar of her drab-gray blouse, she dabbed a few drops of the fragrance on her neck and scooted into the bedroom.

Vern sniffed the air like a Grizzly. Following the scent, his eyes were drawn to Aurelia's body as she loosened her long hair and laid out on the bed. He grinned widely, bits of steak still in his teeth. That didn't bother Aurelia. She loved it when he smiled. To her, he was the most handsome and righteous man she had ever met.

She seductively stroked the blanket next to her thighs, enticing an additional appetite of her husband's. He prided himself as an upright and potent man, both of which he was feeling now. The steak still settling in his stomach, Pastor Vern ripped off his shirt and pounced on Aurelia. Surely his other heavenly mission could wait a bit longer.

PASADENA, CALIFORNIA

ENRIQUE THALIB WORSHIPPED the same God, but he bowed in a different direction. A graduate in computer science from U.C.L.A., he was one of the Islamic Party of God's best assets.

While the rest of the country mourned, Enrique celebrated. A mortal blow had been delivered to the capital of the Great Satan, and for that he praised God. He only wished that he had been a part of it.

He finished his afternoon prayers and checked his e-mail. One of the messages was in code, so Enrique knew it could come from only one man—at least he assumed it was a man. He knew nothing of his commander, except that he was well placed within the international business community.

"Be prepared to infiltrate a rapidly growing movement known as Many Voices of Faith," it read. "Your mission will be to gain access to its leader, Dr. Peter Hart." It ended only with "further instructions will be given to you tomorrow."

Enrique's body shook with excitement. He bit his upper lip as his right leg bounced up and down under the small desk in his studio apartment. He had waited two years for this moment, to again serve the cause, and his God. And now it had arrived.

A short man in his late twenties, he had left home in Indonesia at eighteen after training there with an Islamic militant group. He was fluent in Spanish due to his Filipino mother; his doctored passport was also from the Philippines.

His religion and his politics were well-guarded secrets. As far as his neighbors knew, Enrique was a patriotic Hispanic immigrant and church-going Catholic.

He smiled as he cleaned his silencer. Tomorrow was another mission, an opportunity to glorify God. He closed his eyes and imagined how Muhammad must have felt when he visited Allah in heaven. With His blessing, this psychologist would be easy pickings.

COLORADO

DEEP IN A BUNKER somewhere under the Rocky Mountains, Karen Huffington made her rounds. The loss of her husband and two children back in Washington slowed her gait, but not her determination to serve her country.

"Mr. President," she began hesitantly. It was only the day after the disaster, and she, like the rest of the country, still thought of her boss as the vice president. "Senator Matthews is on line one."

"Good. Patch him through," he responded. A big man with a weathered face and a strong but gentle persona, he had mellowed with age during two terms in the Senate. In addition, his three years as a prisoner of war in Vietnam had strengthened his character and faith early on. If ever there was a vice president ready to assume control during a national crisis, John Norton was the man.

"Todd," he jumped in. He liked the senior senator from Michigan, even though Matthews was a Democrat. "I need you here," he began. John Norton was not a man to mince words. "What with the Speaker and most of the cabinet dead, the country needs to see us united. How soon can you get here?"

"Tell me where, and I'll be there as soon as I can," answered the Senate Majority Leader. Senator Matthews had battled Norton's boss on any number of occasions, but he had worked closely with the vice president when they had served in the Senate together, and he respected his integrity.

"I'll have Karen send a plane for you." He wrote her a note while he switched to speakerphone. "Meanwhile, let's put our heads together on how we want to respond to this thing."

The new president gazed at a picture of his wife. She, like Karen's family, had been killed by the blast. Thank God, he thought to himself, that at least the children were away at college.

"Todd, obviously we've got to punish the people responsible for this attack. And by God, we will," he added, as he picked up the picture of his wife and cradled it in his right hand.

"But we've got to think long term as well," he continued, glancing at a sketch his wife had drawn of the kids. His body went limp as he thought of the millions of children in his country and around the world who needed to be protected. "We've got to continue to be bullish about stopping the spread of weapons of mass destruction, but we also need to build some genuine bridges of understanding between the West and the emerging Islamic world. Otherwise, this madness will keep escalating."

Senator Matthews was encouraged. The previous president was nine parts saber, one part olive branch. This sounded more balanced, and in Matthews' opinion, more likely to work over the long haul.

"I couldn't agree more, Mr. President," he responded. "Your choice of words, 'bridges of understanding,' is already happening through the churches. Have you heard about Peter Hart's news conference in New York, the one with Cardinal O'Conner and the other religious leaders?"

"I did, as a matter of fact. Even checked with our CIA folks on Hart. He's clean." He again glanced over at the picture of his wife. Dr. Hart's movement would have been just the thing Nancy would have loved.

"Couldn't support him officially, of course. My conservative wing would kill me. Besides, we have no way of controlling where he'll take this thing. But unofficially, I'm all for it. As I said, we need those bridges of understanding."

The Senate Majority Leader smiled. Perhaps there is hope, he thought to himself. He wasn't sure how the new president would respond, but he decided to level with him.

"I e-mailed Dr. Hart earlier today. I'm going to introduce a resolution proclaiming June 11th a National Day of Understanding."

Norton was silent for a moment, digesting the news. "I have no problem with that," he responded, much to Matthews' relief. "Unofficially, you have my support. Officially? Well, let's just say I won't oppose it."

"General Collier on line two," interrupted Karen.

"Todd, I've got to take a call. We'll talk more when you get here." Then, his military background showing, "Watch your back on your way here. We can't afford to lose you."

Chapter Six

Wednesday, May 12th—New York

"HEY, YOU THE TV doctor," said the cab driver in broken English, as Peter filed in behind Rabia and the Unity minister. The young man smiled, revealing several empty gaps where teeth once grew.

Peter nodded and returned the smile. He was used to being recognized in public.

"Where to?" asked the driver, his accent now sounding more Arabic, which was confirmed to Peter when he scanned the man's ID card.

Peter looked at Susan Crane for direction. She chimed in with "The Unity Church at 213 West 58th Street."

Gamal put the Ford into gear and headed up First Avenue away from the U.N. building. "I just hear you on radio," he said, making eye contact with Peter in the rearview mirror. "You good man, doctor." Stopping for a red light, over his right shoulder he added, "My family cries for what happened in Washington, but we also afraid."

"These are scary times, my friend," Peter sympathized.

"After 9/11, they threw dirt at my daughter when she walk home from school," shared the driver. He shook his head and sighed. "The world is getting crazier, doctor."

"I am very sorry about your family, Gamal," Peter responded, feeling guilty. He had been so preoccupied with the planet, he had forgotten about the backlash that would surely take place in the United States.

Gamal again made eye contact in the mirror. "Thank you, doctor. But you must be careful, too."

"How so?" asked Peter, treating the young man as an equal, a quality he had garnered over the years as a reporter.

The light turned green, giving the cabby a moment to collect his thoughts. "Many do not want to listen to voice of others. They afraid to lose their way," he answered. Peter attended the driver's discourse as if the cabby were an Egyptian pharaoh. "It be like listening to Satan," Gamal added hesitantly.

The cabby's concern was an obstacle Peter recognized. It was also one he needed to better understand. "For some it is threatening to listen," Peter reflected. "It takes faith to be open, and courage to be vulnerable."

"You wise and kind man, doctor," Gamal replied. Then, "It too bad my brother in Cairo not have this faith and courage you speak of. His faith angry. His courage attacks."

Rabia agreed, in Arabic, which surprised the young man. What astonished him even more was when Peter acknowledged understanding Rabia.

"You speak Arabic, doctor?" he asked with a mixture of bafflement and delight.

"Yes," Peter responded. "My mother was from Cairo. And my father, you should know, drove a cab here for a year just as you do now."

The cabby was so astounded that he pulled over to the side after turning onto 57th Street so he could look directly at Peter. "No kidding," he said, his brown eyes now wide and smiling.

Peter enjoyed the young man's amazement. He also wanted Rabia to know more about him as well, so he continued. "My father met my mother during WW II when he fought the Germans in North Africa. She was Muslim; he was a Jew from New York."

Peter wondered if Rabia recalled their year together at Reed as well as he did. Had she remembered that he understood Arabic? More importantly, had she felt the same attraction back then, or was it only from his side—a student's puppy love for a teacher?

He was pleased when she said, "I remember our chats in Arabic. Do you also speak Hebrew?"

"*Ktzat*," he replied. Peter translated by holding his index finger an inch over his thumb to signal the word little.

"So are you Muslim or Jewish?" she continued, letting her curiosity and passion for inquiry get the better of her.

"*Shwaya, shwaya*," he answered jokingly, which in Arabic meant slowly, slowly. Rabia and the cabby smiled. "I'm only kidding," Peter said. "It's not every day a reporter like me, and a shrink to boot, gets to *answer* personal questions rather than *ask* them, and from such a beautiful interviewer."

"It's getting a bit steamy back here, Gamal," joked Susan. The cabby laughed as he pulled up in front of her church.

"Your Day of Understanding, doctor," Gamal said as they exited the cab. "I will tell all my friends and relations. Allah be with you," he grinned his toothless smile. Then with a reverent nod he bid them "*Salaam*," an Arabic blend of peace and good-bye, and disappeared into traffic on the busy one-way street.

Susan showed Peter and Rabia the church and set them up in a surprisingly large office. "You've got fax, phones, and computers at your service," she said, making a grand sweep of the room with her arm. "So make yourselves at home. We had several folks volunteer to help," she added.

"Thanks," replied Peter, rolling up his sleeves. "Things are happening fast. I have a feeling we'll need all the help we can get."

THE PRESIDENT'S OFFICE, COLORADO

PRESIDENT NORTON WALKED quickly through the underground bunker that was now his home. He needed to sleep, but events needed him more.

He had just completed two meetings—one with his recovery team and another to coordinate the domestic response—and was entering the brightly lit War Room to deal with the international arena. Ten senior military and political advisors seated around a large conference table rose to greet him. "Please, everyone be seated," he told them.

"Mr. President," began General Collier. With the Secretary of Defense also killed during the attack, it was up to him as chairman of the Joint Chiefs to coordinate the response. A distinguished, graying African American, he was as physically strong as he was politically powerful, even at seventy. John Norton respected Joe Collier's strength and relied on his judgment.

"We have both good news and bad coming out of the Islamic world," Collier continued.

"Give me the bad news first."

"I'm going to pass the ball to Ken to fill you in on that score," Collier answered. All eyes shifted to a trim man in a tan suit. CIA Director Ken Sizemore nodded in respect to Collier, then took a deep breath as he turned his head toward the president.

"Sources tell us that the Islamic Party of God may have several more nuclear weapons," said Sizemore.

"Jesus Christ," exclaimed Norton, wincing his right eye and shaking his head. "Do we know where they are?" Then turning to Collier: "Can we take these bastards out?"

"We're working on it, Mr. President," the general replied in an even tone.

"I'm sure you are, Joe," said Norton, regaining his composure. "OK, what have we got so far?" he continued, looking again at Sizemore, his tone now solemn but businesslike.

"The nukes probably were stolen from the Russians and smuggled through Turkestan and Iran, sir," Sizemore responded. "We're working closely with the Russians on this. We'll get these bastards, sir," he added.

"We have to Ken. Failure's not an option here," said Norton, his voice flat like steel. "Keep me abreast of developments, and I mean immediately," he commanded. "I want to hear about things the minute they come in."

The president paused, relaxed his jaw, and turned to Collier. "You mentioned good news, Joe. Hard to imagine, but we can certainly use some. What's the silver lining here?"

The general nodded then gracefully extended his right arm in the direction of a well-groomed woman in a gray pants suit. "Joanna, if you please," he said, handing the floor to one of the few Democratic holdovers from the previous administration.

Joanna Ryburn, second in command at the state department, was well prepared to assume the mantle of Secretary of State after her boss was killed in the attack. A career diplomat, she had served for a while in Lebanon and was fluent in Arabic. There was no love lost between her and CIA Director Sizemore.

"Gentlemen," she began, the only woman at the table. "Obviously we need to track down these murderers and bring them to justice." She looked at the president, then at Sizemore. "And surely that, along with this additional threat to our national security, must be our immediate concerns." The director of the CIA agreed, pressing his thin lips together in a smile.

"However," she added, "we also have a small window of opportunity here to build new bridges between us and the Islamic world." Sizemore smirked. He glanced over at the president and looked surprised when the former fighter pilot and prisoner of war nodded in agreement.

"Moderate fundamentalists are both aghast at and ashamed of what has been committed in the name of Allah," the former Rhodes scholar from Harvard continued, speaking with an eloquence that matched her strong sense of purpose. Sizemore fingered a file in his briefcase. He had the dirt on her; the only question was when to dump it.

"In short," Ryburn summarized, "we can forge a new and cogent alliance with the moderate forces of Islam, and use that as a potent weapon to defeat militant extremists like the Islamic Party of God—but the window will close shortly." Then, glancing at Sizemore, "and tightly if we overreact."

The director of the CIA turned red, his hands clenching into taut fists on the table. "Mr. President, with all due respect to Ms. Ryburn," he interrupted, barely containing his contempt.

"That's *Dr.* Ryburn," she smiled demurely, smelling a battle brewing and not about to yield ground.

"Excuse me, *doctor*," Sizemore bowed his head in feigned deference, his disdain controlled but locked and loaded.

Then turning his attention back to the president: "Surely, sir, our time would be better spent saving our republic rather than weakening it. How can we talk about building bridges with these maniacs when they've murdered so many and are plotting more evil against us." He glared at Ryburn. "We have the high ground politically and morally. We should take advantage of it."

Norton nodded in agreement. "Your point's well taken, Ken." Then looking at Ryburn he added, "And so is yours, Joanna."

The president deliberately made eye contact one by one with the others at the table. "Which is why we're going to extend to the Islamic world both the carrot and the stick."

He rolled up his sleeves and prepared to explain. "We *must* protect against and prevent future acts of terrorism. Those who pursue the path of violence will be dealt with severely. That's the stick, and I intend to use it," said Norton with his trademark sense of conviction.

"But it's also in our national interest to build bridges of understanding between us and the Islamic world. There can be no long term security when the majority of their young people believe we are the Great Satan. The carrot will be our willingness to genuinely connect with them."

He stood up, and the entire table rose with him. President Norton had just formalized his response to the crisis. It was news to him as well as his makeshift cabinet.

THE WEST BANK

HALF A WORLD AWAY, Ahmed Sourani and his two oldest sons dressed for morning prayers. He was far from the halls of power, but his heart was heavy with the tragedy that had befallen the world.

A farmer outside the town of Tulkarem, Ahmed lived with his wife and four children only a few miles from the Israeli border. He and his younger brother and sister had grown up in a Palestinian refugee camp not far away. Most of Ahmed's friends and family were sympathetic to the current intifada, the popular uprising against Israeli rule, although his brother Khalid was the most militant.

Ahmed envied his Jewish neighbors for their tractors when all he had was a mule with which to till the soil. His days were long, and he wanted more for his children, the two oldest of whom worked the arid land alongside him, and who now walked the short mile into town with their father.

"Abu," began his older son Raji. He loved everything about Ahmed, even the word father. "Why are you sad?" asked the twelve-year-old. "Don't we hate the Americans for their evil ways?"

"Yes, my son," he patted Raji on the head. "But somewhere in America there are thousands and thousands of children, like you and Sari, who are dead or dying because of this hatred." He now tousled the younger boy's hair as he continued. "Our holy freedom fighters, the *mujahidin,* have gone too far."

They reached the mosque and took off their shoes. Mullah Abbas, their bearded and aging spiritual leader, began the call to prayer. They bowed low and toward the Kaaba, Islam's holiest of shrines located in Mecca, and recited prayers from the sacred Koran.

Tears filled Ahmed's eyes and fell from his cheeks as he pictured the many innocent children who perished in the blast. He knew that his sons were watching, but these were good tears, and he wanted them to see. Someday he would explain to them how such weeping cleansed prayer rugs and helped wash away the sins of the world.

After morning prayers, Ahmed and the other men talked with their religious leader. "Mullah, does not God tell us 'to slay those who ascribe divinity to aught beside God wherever you may come upon them?'" asked one man, reciting from the Koran.

The mullah gazed thoughtfully at the rolling hills to the east. "But is He also not 'the most merciful?'" he asked.

He looked at Ahmed's two sons and his mouth formed a sad smile. "Are we to keep killing the children of the world?" he asked softly. "My brothers, it is time to make *jihad* within ourselves, as such struggle was originally intended, and less with the Israelis and the Americans."

He unfolded a copy of an Arabic newspaper published in Jerusalem. "Rabia writes that it is time to make peace with our brothers," he added emphatically. He fumbled with his glasses, for at seventy-six it was hard to read such fine print. Finger pointed toward the heavens, he read from her column a verse she had highlighted from the Koran: "That which was given to Moses, and Jesus, and the Prophets, of their Lord, we make no division between any of them."

The men respected Rabia because she was admired by their mullah, and they considered thoughtfully her words from the Koran.

"She says," Mullah Abbas continued, waving the article before him, "that a Day of Understanding is coming throughout the world, and I agree. We must reach out and learn that we are many voices of faith, all children of Allah."

He posted Rabia's column outside the mosque. Ahmed and the others gathered around to read it. There was considerable dissension, but many of the men voted to join Mullah Abbas in a pilgrimage to Jerusalem on the Day of Understanding.

Ahmed smiled as he headed for home with his sons. Allah's mercy and compassion might yet guide the world to safety, and he would play his part.

One of the other men, however, was far from smiling. He waited until the rest left, ripped Rabia's column from the wall, and angrily stuffed it in his pocket. A member of the Islamic Party of God, he vowed a pilgrimage of a different color, as he stalked off into the hills to show the column to his commander.

Chapter Seven

Wednesday, May 12th—
Unity Church, New York

PETER AND RABIA'S large corner office looked like the headquarters of a disaster relief campaign rather than a church conference room. Phones were ringing and faxes poured in by the minute as eight volunteers typed e-mails, answered calls, and placed colored pins on maps covering the walls to reflect responses from around the world.

"I can't believe it was only yesterday morning when this thing happened," said a well-groomed woman in her late seventies, as she doled out slices of pizza for dinner. "It's just now sinking in."

Peter looked up from his computer and sighed. "Unbelievable," he echoed. "So much pain in so short a time. I still can't grasp it."

She nodded. "It's like I'm fine for a while, and then wham, it hits me." She rattled the pizza box with both hands. "Then all I can do is sit down and stare at the wall."

She shook her head and handed him a slice. "Thank God I'm doing this, otherwise I'd go crazy," she said over her shoulder as she wandered off to feed the rest of her newly adopted tribe.

Rabia's column had ignited a firestorm of debate within the Islamic world. Father Ricardo, a retired priest from Mexico City, was coordinating an equally big response from Europe and the Vatican. Peter was especially excited to have Senator Matthews rallying what was left of Congress to proclaim June 11th a National Day of Understanding.

Ministerial associations in Dallas, Atlanta, Boston, Chicago, Seattle, and San Francisco were organizing huge rallies for the coming Sunday. Other major cities were not far behind. The national government, including President Norton, had worried at first about large gatherings, but concluded that they might provide anxious residents with hope, which could help prevent panic and a massive exodus from the nation's urban centers.

Susan Crane, the Unity minister, had been spearheading many of those rallies. Her eyes were ablaze as she pulled up a chair to join Peter and Rabia. "Why don't you take this thing on the road?" she said. "Thousands, perhaps millions of people all across the country would love to support you."

Peter looked at Rabia, who seemed uncertain but open to the idea, then back at Susan. "What do you have in mind?"

"My cousin has an RV rental business in San Diego. He says he's at your disposal if you need him. Why not tour the country?" she beamed, extending her arms out wide as if offering the world. "We can coordinate things from here," she added, her eyes sweeping the room. "You'll have huge turn-outs wherever you go."

Peter liked the idea. As a reporter, he knew how local media hungered for connections to national stories. Susan's image of huge crowds also conjured up Gandhi's march to the sea, but was Peter's intent pure, like Gandhi's?

It was the same guilt he had wrestled with at the news conference. As he often told clients in therapy, we're not terribly complex creatures; usually it's the same theme or two that comes back to haunt us. The image haunting him at the moment was Peter standing on a piano in kindergarten after his mom had been taken away. Nowadays he appeared on network television: a more appropriate way to gain recognition, perhaps, but were its roots much different, or more honorable? Was he still grandstanding for attention, even now?

After asking Susan and Rabia for a moment to reflect, he closed his eyes, and waited for guidance. The Light or Presence, sometimes he referred to it as Spirit, or the Holy Spirit, or God, showed itself—or, as Peter increasingly believed, *he* was more quick to connect with *it,* for surely "It" was always there.

He breathed slowly for two or three minutes, aware that the others were waiting, but he was flourishing enough in his faith not to hurry the process, and desperate enough for answers. *When will I see the world through Your eyes,* he asked God, *and not through ego?*

As he watched the light within grow brighter, he reminded himself to let go of all thought. To hear the answer, he would have to clear out the clutter. He would also have to let go of his preoccupation with himself and replace it with an abiding, heartfelt compassion for others.

Then, from somewhere underneath, like a deep, hidden spring, whispered the still small voice of God. "That's it Peter," it murmured. "Feel the love, and let that guide you. When the *we* replaces *I,* then your eyes will be my eyes."

Peter's breath took him deeper into the Presence as a wave of love traveled up his spine and stained the waters of his consciousness clear. He would trust the voice and let go of all fear. It had passed his litmus test, for it had spoken in love.

He opened his eyes and grinned at Rabia and Susan. His smile was quietly joyous, and his eyes radiated a warm knowing. Rabia nodded yes before Peter even asked. He beamed back, a co-conspirator in silence. Then breaking the stillness, he said to Susan, "We'd love to go; it's a great idea."

"Dr. Hart, line four," shouted one of the volunteers. "It's your daughter, Terra."

Peter brightened, then grew worried. Was she all right? he wondered. "Hi sweetie," he said, squeezing the phone between his neck and left shoulder as he saved an e-mail he was working on to Senator Matthews. "Is everything OK?"

"Dad, you worry too much, especially for a psychologist," she teased. "I promised I'd call, remember?"

"Yeah, but I thought you'd call sooner. It's hard not to worry; you're all I have left," he whined, immediately hating himself for laying that on her.

"Everything's fine, dad," she replied sternly, but he could tell that underneath she resented the pressure. It annoyed her when he put his needs first—at her expense. And yet here he was doing it again. She had a right to be angry. She and Marisa had been distant seconds, especially when it came to his career.

"I want to come to New York and help with your Day of Understanding," she continued. Despite her anger, Peter wasn't surprised that she still wanted to join him. Since Marisa's death, he was all she had, too. "I can't concentrate on school since the attack anyway."

Peter's first thought was to encourage her to finish college. She was close to graduating, and the chair of the psychology department wanted her for the Ph.D. program. He was about to say something fatherly, when Terra sensed what was coming and launched a pre-emptive strike.

"Dad, I don't want any lectures about finishing school."
She knew him almost as well as he knew himself, and her
psychology training made her even more formidable. "Besides," she continued, "*you* dropped out of college to go
logging for a year."

She had him there, Peter realized. "OK," he capitu-
lated, perhaps too easily, he would later lament. "I could
never argue with you anyway." Besides, Peter told himself,
working on such a project would be good experience. The
real reasons, however, were far simpler, but less clear—he
missed her and wanted her safely nearby.

"Thanks daddy," replied Terra, sounding happy and
like a little girl again. "I love you."

"I love you, too, sweetie," he responded. He looked up
self-consciously to see Rabia and Susan smiling proudly at
him, as only women can when they see a man behave tenderly toward his children. He winked, thinking it would
lighten the moment and re-establish his limited machismo,
but they knew better, and it only broadened their smiles.

Then remembering the RV idea, he added, "Terra,
we're probably flying to California, maybe even tonight. So
don't buy a ticket." He looked at his watch and began calcu-
lating a possible flight schedule. "I'll call you within the
hour to let you know what's up."

"OK, daddy. It'll be great to see you."

"It will, indeed. I love you, sweetie." He hung up and
again glanced over at the women. They had opted to give

him his privacy, however, and were busily arranging things with Susan's cousin in San Diego.

He wolfed down the pizza and checked out flights for later that night. The airlines were returning to normal. If only our psyches could be as easy, he bemoaned.

EN ROUTE TO SAN DIEGO

PETER AND RABIA packed quickly and boarded the red-eye from La Guardia. Sixty volunteers would join them in Southern California the following day, most with their own vehicles, although Susan's cousin had generously donated ten RV's to the cause.

Rabia fell asleep soon after takeoff as Peter lost himself in the stars outside his window and the sadness he felt for the tens of thousands who had died or were still suffering. Perhaps a drink would muffle their cries, he thought to himself. Why feel the pain, when he could bottle it up, anesthetize it?

He ordered a Scotch and looked out at the night. A line from the Omaha chief Big Elk surfaced from his subconscious: "Death will come, always out of season." The words had haunted Peter after Marisa died, and they wailed now in his brain as he thought of the many thousands who had lost loved ones in Washington. And for what? he implored. All because we can't get along with one another?

Please God, help us find a way to resolve our differences, he pleaded silently, his sadness pooling into tears. He closed his eyes and went deeper into the stillness. It wasn't long before the Presence came to him.

"You know how to resolve differences, Peter," said the familiar voice. "You must show others."

Peter nodded. Was the voice referring to his role as a psychologist? It didn't matter; what counted was that he had been given a mission, for reasons he might never figure out. With eyes still closed, he waited in the silence. He was less afraid of both the voice and the mission now. The world needed him, and he would play his part.

"I will reveal to you ten new commandments," continued the voice, "although you already know them. It is these you must teach the world."

Peter waited in the darkness, but heard nothing more. He opened his eyes and again looked at the stars. We are so small, he reflected, so insignificant.

At that moment a baby spider, no bigger than the tip of a pen, descended along a thin thread from the top of Peter's window.

"Small, yes," said the inner voice. "But you are all uniquely precious to me, all flowers in my garden—from the tiniest lichen to the tallest sunflower, regardless of size or color. This is the first of my new commandments, Peter. Speak of this tomorrow in San Diego."

Peter wrote down what God had told him. He wondered about the other nine commandments, but he knew that God would reveal them on God's schedule, not his.

He thanked the starry night for its beauty, closed his eyes, and slept deeply. A small bottle of Scotch lay unopened nearby.

SOUTHERN CALIFORNIA

"THE PIGEON ARRIVES in San Diego this morning," began the encrypted message on Enrique's computer. He grinned at the prospect of action as he read the details about Peter's RV tour.

He packed, carefully placing his silencer within the hidden compartment of his bag, and began the two hour drive down the Santa Ana Freeway from his apartment in South Pasadena. As a computer specialist with a large security and surveillance company in Southern California, he had driven it many times, having recently updated the system protecting Sea World.

He struggled to suppress his excitement as he turned into the driveway of the busy RV lot. He parked near the exit and waded into the crowd. Peter was easy to recognize; Enrique often saw him on the news.

"Dr. Peter Hart," he said, extending his hand and smiling. "It's an honor to meet you." Peter smiled back and thanked Enrique for coming. He then introduced him to the others.

They now numbered several hundred, thanks mostly to coverage that morning on Peter's home station in L.A. and the affiliate in San Diego. Perelli had sent Bear down as well to begin covering the caravan for the network on a national level. Perelli's boss, Duncan, hadn't liked the idea, but with approval coming from the very top, Duncan couldn't do much about it. Like it or not, Duncan had been told, Peter was now a story—and a developing one at that.

Enrique was handed to Bear because of the young man's computer and security skills. Due to Bear's experience as a Green Beret and communications specialist in Vietnam, he had taken it upon himself to protect the caravan and his good friend Peter.

"Where you from, Thalib?" asked Bear suspiciously. It was his nature not to trust. Besides his work behind enemy lines during the war, he had grown up in the '50s as one of a handful of blacks in a small Southern town.

"The Philippines," Enrique lied. It was simple enough to do after ten years. "I came to this country to go to college. I have a degree in computer science," he added, smiling. "One of the reasons I was assigned to help you."

It all sounded reasonable enough, thought Bear, and Enrique looked harmless. But there was something about him that Bear couldn't shake. "I'll need a resume and references before we head out," he told him.

"No problem, I've got one in my laptop," Enrique smiled.

Bear looked him up and down, and then checked his car. "Can't give you one of the RV's," he added. "Is this thing going to make it cross-country?"

"Oh, sure." Again the trademark smile. "She's old, but reliable." Enrique patted the hood of his '92 Ford wagon. He was relieved not to be bunking in an RV. It would leave him more undisturbed, and he had learned from previous missions that privacy was crucial.

PETER WINKED AT Bear, who whistled loudly with his fingers. Several hundred heads turned in Peter's direction, and he motioned them to join him.

"Thank you all for coming," he said. He went deeper into the Presence and bowed his head. "Let us begin with a moment of silence," he continued, "to pray and reflect, each in our own way, for the tens of thousands of innocent lives lost in Washington." The lot grew quiet, like a widow at sunset, except for a half dozen reporters and photographers, who went about their business of recording the moment.

Peter waited amidst the sadness until most of the heads had risen from their somber reflection. "This grief we feel for what happened in Washington, including our fear, and anger—what are we to do with these feelings?" he asked. "We can avenge the violence with more violence, but where will that take us?" His voice was earnest as he urged everyone, including himself, to imagine such a journey.

Suddenly, as if permeated by some unseen wellspring of power, his voice rose as he pounded the podium. "Or we can harness our towering anguish, and like a burning torch, use it to light our way through the darkness." His fervor lifted him and his audience from their post-disaster chasm of gloom and despair, at least for the time being.

He paused to collect himself. Breathing slowly, he emptied his mind and soaked in the vintage San Diego day: balmy and cloudless, with only a slight breeze coming in from the sea. He smelled the salt air. A formation of pelicans glided by, as if on cue, which perhaps they were, he considered. "The pelicans here may be different than those that fly along the coast of Saudi Arabia or Indonesia. But are they not equal in the eyes of God?" asked Peter, his sentences coming more through him than from him.

He let his words hang in the air. As he waited for the Presence to breathe more language into him, his eyes fell upon a giant sycamore. Pointing to it, he continued: "Are not the trees in Iran and Yemen also equal in the eyes of the Creator to those here in the United States?"

The crowd again nodded in agreement. This time Peter's gaze focused on the people before him. "Look at us," he directed, slowly waving his right hand over their heads as if to bless them, which in a way he was, for to love is to bless, and he was feeling great love. "As different as *we* all are," he continued, his voice softening, "are *we* not unique flowers in God's garden, each reflecting the Creator's radiance in *our* own unique way?"

The crowd murmured in response as cameras, microphones, and reporters' notebooks captured the brightness of the moment. "It is time to realize, truly realize, that we are all brothers and sisters," he begged, his heart filled with love and sorrow. "We speak in many voices of faith, but we are all children of the Creator. We must learn how to feel that, on levels we haven't felt before." He choked up, but with tenderness, and hope. "For if we are all God's children," he whispered, "and we *feel* that, and *know* that, we will not harm one another."

Then lifted by the energy of the crowd and the passion of his own message, he asked loudly, "Are you with me?"

Several hundred responded with one voice. "Yes."

"Are you with me?" he asked again, lost in the embrace of the moment. This time the answer was louder.

Peter let the noise settle and smiled at the crowd, allowing the silence to linger under the Southern California sun. Then, raising his arms, he asked everyone to join him. "Heavenly Father," he began, feeling the Light flowing through his body.

"God of many names, Great Spirit," he continued, "please be with us as we carry our message across this great country and around the world. Guide us in our actions and infuse us with your love, that we may bring peace to our troubled planet."

He started to sing "Let there be peace on earth, and let it begin with me." It was popular in many churches, so most in the crowd knew it.

Enrique joined hands and sang with the others. Looking up at the heavens, he shut his eyes, and grinned wildly. Peace would come from Allah, he smirked, and he was prepared to be His fiery messenger.

Chapter Eight

Thursday, May 13th—San Diego

PETER'S FACE LIT up in the afternoon sun as Terra bounded up to the RV and jumped into his arms, but there was a touch of sadness in his heart as well. Her long legs and quick gait reminded him of Marisa.

"Hi beautiful," he said, covering his sadness and lowering her to the ground. "You look great."

"Thanks, daddy," Terra answered, still holding his hands. She turned away her bright blue eyes. The bounce ebbed from her body. "I'm sorry," she whispered. "It's just that when I see you, I think of mom."

"I know, sweetie," Peter responded, again pulling her close. "Me too, baby. Me too." He brushed a long lock of curly blond hair off her cheek and lifted her chin with his hand. "You know Keats' line about a thing of beauty being a joy forever?" he asked, his eyes insisting on contact.

She shook her head no, but a smile began to sprout at the corners of her mouth. She loved it when her dad recited poetry.

"Well, what he says next is also important: 'Its loveliness increases; it will never pass into nothingness.' I believe that," he smiled, looking deeply into his daughter's eyes. "At least, I try to," he added, letting her know that to grieve was human, and that they were both still very human.

"Peter," interrupted Rabia's voice from inside the RV. "Where did you put those maps?" She stuck her head out the door and did a double take, her face erupting into a smile. "Terra, you're as beautiful as your picture."

She raced down the steps and gave Terra a hug, but the younger woman stiffened, and looked away.

"Forgive me," Rabia laughed. "We haven't even met, and here I am assaulting you." Then, stepping back, she explained, "We've prepared the back for you; your dad's going to be up over the cab. I'll be in that tan RV behind you," she reassured her, pointing to the other vehicle. "Let me help you with that," she added, extending a tentative hand toward the young woman's suitcase.

Terra smiled politely, but declined. "Thanks, I can manage," she replied. She did allow Rabia to show her inside, however, leaving Peter alone to check under the hood.

He sensed his daughter's ambivalence toward Rabia, and he was surprised at how much he wanted them to get along. His mind drifted back to the British Virgin Islands where he, Terra, and Marisa had sailed the Christmas before

Marisa died. He remembered one particular afternoon at the helm tacking toward the island of Jost Van Dyke while his wife and daughter wrapped a few presents nearby. It was one of those moments Peter knew he'd never forget, and he smiled as he remembered it now.

How beautiful his wife was, even without her hair. The youngest daughter of a Methodist minister, she had taught him the meaning of faith and the joy that comes from being part of a spiritual community. He could almost hear her laugh that day, and the radiance of her face, despite her loss of color, had been unmatched even by the brilliance of the Caribbean Sea.

The doctors had told her that the cancer had spread from her breast to her bones and several of her organs. She had decided to die as she had lived, with laughter in her voice and love in her heart.

Peter recalled the jewelry box her father had carved for her on her thirteenth birthday. On the lid he had engraved, *Her gift in life is being loved; in loving, gives the gift of life.* She would continue to give that gift, not because she was supposed to, but because she didn't know how to live (or die) any other way.

Peter was rattled out of his reverie by raucous giggling coming from Rabia and Terra. It was then he realized how right he felt with Rabia, and how much he needed Terra to accept her. After two long years, the empty seat at the family table might yet be filled, the circle completed, although different. Once again there might be three of them on a journey together, and once again there might be laughter.

THE WEST BANK

IN THE HILLS above Tulkarem, Islamic Party of God commander Khalid Sourani finished morning prayers and joined his wife Tawriya at breakfast.

"Did you finish the uniforms?" he asked, pausing to tickle their three-year-old playing on the floor.

Tawriya smiled proudly and pointed to two Israeli outfits lying on the bed in the alcove by the kitchen. She poured a small cup of coffee and brought it to Khalid.

"The bomb arrives today," he told her, trying not to sound as excited as he felt. "Soon we will liberate Palestine and all of Islam."

"*Inshallah*," God willing, she replied.

Khalid didn't know about New York or London. He did know, however, that a nuclear bomb, smuggled out of Russia through Iran and Syria, had crossed the Jordan River that night and would arrive shortly. Disguising themselves as soldiers, Khalid and Tawriya would drive the bomb into the heart of Tel Aviv using a stolen Israeli jeep hidden in a cave nearby.

Within the first five seconds of its detonation, 200,000 unbelievers would die at ground zero, Khalid reminded himself gleefully. Seconds later, the blast would destroy buildings within a six mile radius. During the next five hours, 300,000 infidels would be injured, half of them severely. Then, salivating at the thought, Israel would retaliate, triggering a holy war that would finally create the Islamic state God had commanded the Prophet Muhammad to establish.

Khalid's attention shifted from Tel Aviv to his more immediate surroundings. "My mother will take care of the children," he reassured Tawriya, pulling her close, although the thought of never seeing their faces again saddened him beyond words. "When the time comes, she will help the little ones understand."

An abrupt knock on the door startled them both. "It's me," shouted Khalid's brother, Ahmed.

They cautiously lifted the latch and invited him in. "What lures you off your farm and into our peaceful hills?" asked Khalid, feigning a smile. He loved his older brother, but he was disgusted with Ahmed's willingness to compromise with the unbelievers.

"I know you have heard about our pilgrimage to Jerusalem on the Day of Understanding," answered Ahmed, accepting a cup of coffee from Tawriya. "Will you join us? Raji and little Sari have asked about you."

"Dear brother, you know how I feel about the Jews," answered Khalid, trying his best not to boil over. "They and the Americans are our enemies. There can be no compromise with Satan," he added, his voice now rising. "How can you even think of such a thing, when they have killed father, and now our little Arin!" he yelled.

Ahmed understood his brother's bitterness. Their father died during the first intifada in 1992, and their younger sister had recently been killed during an Israeli mortar attack. "It is precisely because of all this killing that we must end it," he replied, trying to take Khalid's hands into his. He had hoped that the destruction of Washington would have softened his brother's heart.

Khalid pushed him away and stormed off. As Ahmed watched his brother rant across the kitchen, he noticed the two Israeli uniforms in the alcove nearby. Tawriya quickly threw clothes over them, but it was too late. Although Ahmed pretended not to see anything, Tawriya knew better.

"Well, perhaps I should go," he said, not wanting to upset his brother any further, and not knowing how to deal with what he had seen.

"I'm sorry," apologized Khalid. "But Allah has chosen different paths for us, my brother." He reversed direction and showed him to the door.

"*Mashaallah*," whatever Allah destines to be, answered Ahmed. He already had worried that his brother might be involved in terrorist activities; this only confirmed it.

After Ahmed left, Tawriya told her husband what she had witnessed. "He may know too much," she warned.

Khalid ran to the door, but stopped himself, and pounded the wall with his fists. He couldn't kill his brother, but he wouldn't jeopardize the operation either, not when they were this close to victory.

"We'll keep an eye on him," he responded, "and leave it in Allah's capable hands." His voice was low, but his fists remained hard as rocks.

COLORADO WHITE HOUSE

THE DIRECTOR OF the CIA closed his eyes and placed his hands on the family Bible. Torn by competing ideologies, Ken Sizemore was in turmoil.

On the one hand, he was a decorated Vietnam veteran who swore to uphold the Constitution. His father, a Baptist minister and fighter pilot during World War II, had sent him away to a military academy at the age of five. A graduate of West Point, honor and country were his life.

But he was also deeply religious and had become increasingly fanatical about his beliefs. A Christian Reconstructionist, it was Sizemore's duty to take back the culture from godless liberals, blasphemers and homosexuals. America needed to be rescued, and pluralism meant compromising with the devil.

Push was coming to shove. The Constitution was now pitted against the Bible, as Sizemore understood them. In his view, God gave Adam, and later Noah, Dominion over the earth, so it was up to good Christians like Sizemore to subdue the world and impose Jesus' rule on earth before the Second Coming of Christ.

He asked Jesus for direction and opened the Bible. There the words of Saint Peter glistened as if illuminated by a searchlight. "With a roar the sky will vanish," read the words of the apostle, referring to the last day. "The elements will catch fire and fall apart," the text continued, and "the earth and all that it contains will be burnt up."

The director of the CIA shuddered. These nuclear bombs were part of a larger, divine plan. Christ's return was imminent, and it was up to Sizemore to play his part.

He closed his Bible, kissed it, and returned the precious book to its conspicuous position on the upper right-hand corner of his desk. Grabbing his briefcase, he walked slowly out of his office and down the hall to update the new president and General Collier on the latest intelligence. It was only two days after the attack on Washington, and the CIA director, like many in positions of leadership, hadn't slept more than a few hours.

He waited in the anteroom while the president's secretary buzzed her boss. She returned her attention to Sizemore, nodded, and announced, "the president will see you now."

Sizemore opened the door. Senate Majority Leader Todd Matthews and the new Secretary of State, Joanna Ryburn, were sitting with President Norton at a small conference table in the middle of the office.

"Ken, welcome," hailed the president as he rose to greet the CIA director, the two Democrats rising with him. "Please join us."

Norton liked Sizemore and understood his distaste for liberals. As a moderate Republican, the new president had worked closely for many years with fundamentalist Christians. He applauded their dedication to service and their commitment to family and country, but he was leery of their intolerance and myopic world view.

"I *know* you've met our new Secretary of State," Norton proceeded playfully, swiveling his arm toward Joanna Ryburn. Sizemore and Ryburn tried to smile in keeping with the humorous tone set by Norton but came off looking like two boxers nodding politely during introductions before a fight.

"I'm not sure if you and the Majority Leader have met, however," the president continued, gesturing toward Matthews.

"Yes we have, sir," Sizemore answered politely, as he and Matthews shook hands.

Norton waved the group into chairs.

"We've played basketball together in the basement of the old Senate office building," Sizemore continued. He hesitated for an instant, remembering that the building had been blown away along with everything else in the capital. The others, realizing why he had paused, joined in the impromptu moment of somber reflection.

"Matthews is a team player, sir," added Sizemore, breaking the silence, "and I respect that." The Senate Majority Leader was a moderate, and the director of the CIA admired his willingness to stand up to Hollywood liberals in defense of traditional family values.

The president looked at his watch, then buzzed his secretary to summon General Collier. While they waited, he thanked Matthews and Ryburn for helping him forge a bipartisan response.

"It's important that we not only *appear* united on this thing, but that we *are* united as a nation," he noted, sounding like the world leader he had become only forty-eight hours earlier. "Building bridges of understanding between the West and Islam must go hand in hand with a strong military campaign."

Sizemore winced at the suggestion of compromising with such heathens. He looked at Ryburn and fondled a file in his briefcase.

The president's secretary interrupted the meeting. "Sir, the assistant director of the CIA needs to speak to Mr. Sizemore. He says it's urgent."

"Thanks, Karen." Then to Sizemore, the president said, "You can take it on my line, if you'd like."

Sizemore walked to the phone while the others continued to talk foreign policy. "Colin, what's the latest on those nukes?" he asked.

The room went quiet. They watched as Sizemore answered in clipped tones. "Yes. I see. Hmm. Are you sure? Not good. Thanks, Colin." He hung up slowly and returned to the group like a whipped dog.

General Collier entered the room. The president nodded a quick greeting, and turned again to his CIA director.

"Ken, what's the story?" He could tell it wasn't going to be good.

Sizemore straightened. He looked at Norton with a pained expression. "The Russians confirm that four nuclear bombs were indeed stolen from their arsenal."

Matthews and Ryburn sat stunned. Norton mumbled "son of a bitch," while Collier tightened his jaw, squinting his steel eyes.

"They won't say it publicly, but they believe it was an inside job," Sizemore continued, looking mostly at Norton and Collier. "One of their generals was bought by the Islamic Party of God."

"Do we know where the other nukes are or where they're going?" asked General Collier, his voice matching the gravity of his uniform.

"Our operatives in the Mideast and Europe believe that the intended targets are Tel Aviv, possibly London, and possibly New York."

The Secretary of State gasped, an inclination shared by the men, but held in check through years of gender conditioning—except for the president, who parlayed his fear into anger, slamming his fist on the conference table.

"We'll get these bastards," Norton swore, adding ominously, "by whatever means necessary." His eyes were cold and fixed on Sizemore.

"My sentiments exactly, sir," the director of the CIA responded.

"Joe," snapped the president, looking at General Collier, "I want to see contingency plans a.s.a.p. Joanna, get on the horn with the Russians, the Brits, and the Israelis." An ex-military man, Norton knew how to command in a crisis, and he was on fire. "Ken, we need to know where the hell those nukes are—now. And Todd, you and I have a press conference in ten minutes."

Then, glaring at all of them, he added, "This is on a need to know basis. We can't panic three entire cities." He paused, adding, "at least not yet." He rose and ended the meeting: "I want to hear from each of you within the hour."

The Senate Majority Leader stayed. The others scrambled like firefighters at a four-alarm blaze. As Sizemore rushed out the door, he caught a glimpse of Norton, his brow dark and furrowed, pacing like a panther in a tight cage.

The director of the CIA turned the corner and hurried down the hall. His neck twitched, his breathing was short, and the Biblical admonition, "With a roar the sky will vanish," echoed in his subconscious.

Chapter Nine

Thursday, May 13th— Southern California

PETER'S CARAVAN OF a thousand cars and RVs stretched ten miles along the Santa Ana Freeway, wending its way from San Diego to Los Angeles through the evening rush hour. Helicopters from throughout Southern California clattered overhead covering the scene live for their five o'clock newscasts.

With the world in chaos, Peter enjoyed the illusion of control he felt while driving. It was still only day three since the attack on Washington, so he wasn't surprised that most of the stories remained about the recovery effort in D.C. and the nation's political and military response. He *was* surprised, however, to hear the motorcade featured within the first news block on several television broadcasts and to field so many live radio interviews, one of which he was in the middle of now.

"Dr. Hart," asked the anchor of L.A.'s most popular station, "what do you say to the millions of Americans who want revenge for what the Islamic extremists did in Washington?"

The power of the media rarely failed to impress Peter, even though he was a veteran. Here he was driving on one of the nation's busiest freeways—his daughter riding shotgun, his right hand on the steering wheel, his left elbow perched out the window—talking into a headset to hundreds of thousands of listeners, some in vehicles right next to him.

"First of all," he responded, "and this is pretty obvious, we need to recognize that our anger is totally understandable. How could we not be furious in the face of such tragedy, and such villainy?"

"So it's natural," fed back the anchor.

"Absolutely," reinforced Peter, "and most of us know that. We've been abused, big time, and we're mad as hell about it. The research, incidentally, shows that we react stronger when disasters are manmade, like when a dam fails, as opposed to acts of God, like a hurricane or an earthquake. And if it's intentional, as opposed to accidental, the anger is deeper and lasts longer."

Terra gave her dad a thumbs-up and smiled proudly.

"Interesting," replied the anchor. "This, of course, is both. And then there's the sheer magnitude of the attack as well. So essentially, then, revenge is understandable."

"The *desire* for revenge is understandable," explained Peter. "How we cope with that feeling—that's another matter."

"So you're saying we shouldn't exact an eye for an eye, even though, psychologically, the urge is natural?" the anchor asked, somewhat skeptically.

"Exactly. Revenge is one thing. Justice, however, is something else again. We should clarify, by the way, that Many Voices of Faith isn't a peace movement," he continued, "at least in the short term. It's about promoting understanding over the long haul."

"So you're not necessarily against the use of force?" questioned the anchor, sounding surprised by Peter's answer.

"Not if used wisely. Clearly we need to prevent such attacks and put an end to the proliferation of weapons of mass destruction," explained Peter. He believed in using force to prevent aggression, despite it sounding like a contradiction in terms, especially to his more liberal followers.

"But religious intolerance is today's greatest obstacle to world peace," he added. He knew that the expressions *religious intolerance* and *world peace* were red flags for many conservatives, and he hesitated to alienate anyone, but both were at the heart of his mission. "Which is why we are attempting to build bridges of understanding between us and the Islamic world."

"Were you aware," the anchor interrupted, somewhat excitedly, "that President Norton just talked about building such bridges of understanding only moments ago, when he and the Senate Majority Leader outlined what's being called America's carrot and stick doctrine?"

"It's an idea whose time has come," agreed Peter. He disliked clichés, but he respected their clarity and their power to communicate. "In fact," he continued, "Senator Matthews is proposing that Congress declare June 11th, the one month anniversary of the attack on Washington, a National Day of Understanding."

The anchor, sounding delighted to get the scoop, wished the caravan well and informed listeners that Peter would address the crowd, already estimated at 5,000, later that evening at City Hall.

A red SUV next to Peter honked, as a large lady wearing silver-tinted sunglasses riding shotgun rolled down her window and yelled, "Go get 'em, doc." She encircled her mouth with her hands like a megaphone and bellowed, "We're gonna' pick up my husband's mother and join you over at City Hall."

Peter smiled and shouted back, "Thanks for helping." He waved as the SUV honked again, picked up steam and moved on.

"That's why *I'm* here daddy—to help," Terra joined in from her perch in the passenger seat. "I felt so powerless after the attack. Now I feel like I'm doing something."

"Funny how I didn't appreciate that until now," Peter reflected. "I guess a lot of people felt the same way I did when I sent off that first e-mail."

"Dad," Terra continued, the questioning lilt in her voice sounding more personal.

"Yeah, sweetie," he responded cautiously.

"I'd like to switch places with Rabia."

"What do you mean?" asked Peter, puzzled by her choice of words.

"Well, I know you like her," continued Terra carefully. "And although it's not easy seeing you with another woman, I can tell she likes you, too."

"Oh?" answered Peter, partly as a father, but mostly now as a lonely man hearing that love, unlike lightening, perhaps could strike twice. "And just how can you tell that?" he teased, the raw curiosity in his voice, however, not escaping his daughter.

"Oh, come on daddy!" she laughed. "Honestly, you men can be so blind," she scolded, sounding more like a woman than a twenty-one year old girl. "I see the way she looks at you. She's madly in love with you!"

Peter's face waxed from confused to happy, but soon waned to serious. "Do you really think so?" he asked, no longer the father but a befuddled older man seeking advice from a younger woman.

"Dad, trust me on this one," she reassured him, sensing his vulnerability. "Also," she added, again choosing her words, "I want you to be happy." She reached over and squeezed his shoulder. "It's OK to go for it, dad."

Peter was surprised at how liberating it felt to get his daughter's permission. He knew about her anger, how she had felt cheated by him when he would answer the siren call of broadcasting rather than stay close to hearth and home. How many men had he counseled about the delicate balance between family and career, only to fail in his own pursuit of that same elusive quarry.

He turned and looked at her. His watery eyes thanked her more than his words, although he did manage to squeak out "Thanks, sweetie."

They sat together amidst the cacophony of car engines and helicopters. "It's OK to have Rabia drive with you," continued Terra. "I can drive her RV, or if you prefer, I can go with Bear or Enrique."

Peter was surprised at her mention of Enrique. Bear was like an uncle to her, but how did she know Enrique?

Terra, sensing her father's surprise, pre-empted his question. "He helped me and Rabia earlier," she reported, "and he offered to drive me to L.A." She shot him a look of disgust. "Dad, don't get weird on me now. You're always so paranoid when it comes to men!"

Her broadside made Peter wince. "I know, sweetie. I'm sorry," he apologized. "Look, you're a big girl now. I'll leave that up to you."

Shifting to a more appreciative vein, he reached over and squeezed her hand. "Your approval of Rabia means a lot to me, sweetie. Thanks." A wry smile journeyed from his mouth to his eyes, causing them to sparkle. "So coach," he grinned, "how do I ask Rabia to be my RV buddy?"

Terra returned the smile. Then parroting his words back at him, she chuckled, "You're a big boy, daddy. I'll leave that up to you."

PETER PULLED UP to City Hall and was taken back by the size of the crowd, as ten to fifteen thousand cheered his arrival, some waving placards saying "Many Voices of Faith" and "A Day of Understanding."

He was humbled by the response, as people continued to stream in from every corner. "Give me twenty minutes to center myself," he asked Bear, as he climbed into the RV to meditate.

"You got it," Bear replied, posting himself outside the door. With his shades, black skintight T-shirt, and large tattoo on his right shoulder, he made a formidable bodyguard. The big man searched his buddy's face and added, "You can do this, doc."

Peter smiled and relaxed his shoulders. He saw Rabia through the window and blew her a kiss as he walked to the rear of the RV. She gleamed back, folded her hands together in a prayerful gesture, and nodded.

Reassured by his companions, Peter closed his eyes and entered the silence. With each breath, he drifted deeper. There he waited like a patient lover.

"The humility you felt when you saw the crowd," said the now familiar voice within, "*that* is the second commandment."

Peter lingered in the unruffled stillness. "*You* know how limited the human mind is," God continued, again referring to Peter's training as a psychologist. "Remind others to proceed humbly."

Peter nodded, took a slow breath, and waited for the next tide of the Presence to fill him.

"My universe is beyond understanding," came the voice, sailing in on Peter's next breath. "Always remember that human glasses are limited and often stained with prejudice."

Peter felt the equanimity of God's gentleness enfold him. "I am love, Peter, not hatred—an open hand, not a closed fist."

Peter sensed that God was finished, but waited, humbly, in case he was wrong. After a few minutes, he opened his eyes. He had his marching orders.

Faith, not fear, he reminded himself as he proceeded with Bear and Rabia toward the podium. He gazed out over a sea of faces; camera crews and reporters from around the country bobbed in front of him.

The crowd, now numbering 20,000, quieted as if a giant hand had waved a wand over it. He stood in front of them for what seemed like minutes, then raised his arms like he was bestowing a blessing. "Let us pray," he began, "each in our own way."

He closed his eyes and quieted his mind, emptying it of all thought. This would come from God, he vowed, or it wouldn't come at all. Ego was not going to run *this* show.

"Great and Holy Spirit, God of many names, we ask for your guidance and your love," he proceeded, although it was unclear to Peter who was speaking, him or Spirit.

"We pray to you with many voices of faith," continued the detached voice from a deeper source. "And we ask that you help us hear one another's common humanity, that we may build bridges of understanding between our different beliefs.

"In this moment of silence, we pray, too, that your guidance and your love will comfort the friends and family of those killed and wounded in Washington, D.C." Peter paused, as the silence of 20,000 was beamed across the country and around the world.

He opened his eyes and saw Rabia smile and nod. Her love and spiritual companionship emboldened his faith and strengthened his resolve. He took a breath to center himself, slowly exhaled, and continued.

"Earlier today in San Diego we reaffirmed that each of us is a precious child of the universe," he reminded the gathering, his voice gaining power and momentum, "a unique flower in God's garden, regardless of our name for God.

"This evening I say that we must move ahead with great humility, for while God sees the whole picture, we humans see only pieces of it, and biased ones at that."

He searched the hearts of the people below and felt their longing for hope, and peace, and God, all of which they saw in him. How ironic, he reflected, that while he was preaching humility, they were baptizing him as a new spiritual leader. He took an extra breath to ensure that Spirit would inform his message, not ego.

"What's happening right now?" he asked, pausing to give the assemblage a chance to entertain the question. "You're listening to my words, each of you hearing them differently. The photographers are busy lining up their shots," he continued, looking into the cameras and gesturing toward the press with an open hand. "The police in front are worrying about security."

He let the moment linger, his point beginning to sink in. "The bottom line is that while God sees the whole picture, you and I experience only snippets, and different ones at that.

"So what does this mean?" he challenged, again letting his words hang in the air. "It means that you and I do *not* have a corner on truth, only tiny pieces of it, and so we need to proceed humbly."

Peter paused again, not for dramatic effect, but simply to look at the audience. There was an old lady in a red hat, a young father holding a baby, and a businessman, probably from an office building nearby, still wearing his coat and tie. He smiled at the variety of faces and garb.

"We are each so uniquely complicated," he continued. "Did you know," he teased, "that the human brain has 100 billion neurons. If you calculated the number of ways those brain cells could combine to form different thoughts, including the different ways we're experiencing this very moment, and wrote out that number, according to one scientist, it would fill a 500-page book—100 million times."

The lady with the red hat dropped her jaw, while the businessman next to her squinted his eyes, straining to absorb the calculation.

"So how should we proceed to share our many voices of faith—Christian, Jew, Muslim, or Hindu?" he asked rhetorically. Wrapping up his sermon for the evening, he answered, "Gently, and with great humility."

Then, in what would become a standard ending for Peter, he shouted "God bless you. God bless America. And God bless the world's many voices of faith."

The young father started singing "God Bless America." The crowd eagerly joined him. Peter's movement had caught the nation's attention.

ELBURZ MOUNTAINS, IRAN

IT ALSO CAUGHT the attention of Peter's distant cousin, Vladimir. He had limped his way over rocky terrain for a day-and-a-half before stumbling onto a well-stocked cabin not far from the nearby town of Tankabon a few hours after sunrise. There he learned about the destruction of Washington on CNN and was shocked to see Peter addressing the masses in Los Angeles.

He immediately dialed Peter's number. Because of his experiences with the KGB, he still didn't trust Russian authorities. "You must help me," he pleaded into Peter's answering machine. "They have Katerina and little Ivan, and they have threatened to kill them. They may also have three more bombs, Peter. We must stop them."

Vladimir had just left the cabin's phone number when he heard a noise outside the window. He quickly shut off the TV and hung up the phone. He grabbed a stool sitting near the television and tiptoed to the door. Raising it over his head, he waited for the door to open. It didn't.

After a few minutes of considerable turmoil, Vladimir lifted the latch on one of the windows and crawled out. He was immediately bumped from behind. Whirling savagely he swung the stool, landing a solid blow on the fly-infested flank of a large cow. He collapsed in a mixture of nervous laughter and adrenaline as the animal bolted away in a frenzied search for a more peaceful pasture.

Vladimir staggered back in and wrote down the names of the madmen who had stolen the bombs and where they were likely taking them. It was a slow process; he had not slept or eaten since his escape. He stretched out on the sofa for a moment and closed his eyes. He laid there like a dead man for the next three hours.

The phone's ring cut through Vladimir like a sharp Siberian wind, shattering his sleep and rattling his already fragile nerves. His eyes inspected the cabin. Then remembering where he was and who might be calling, he lunged for the phone, snatching it up before the third ring.

"Peter?" he asked, praying it would be his cousin and not his captors. He had grown close to Peter since their first meeting soon after the collapse of the Soviet Union.

Their grandparents were brother and sister and had remained devoted to each other, even after Peter's grandmother emigrated to the United States. Vladimir had wondered whether it was the story of their family's reunion, popularized by the media both in the United States and in Russia, that first alerted the Islamic Party of God to his role as a nuclear scientist. But none of that mattered now, as Vladimir's body let out a deep sigh hearing Peter's voice.

"Vlad," apologized Peter, calling him by the nickname he had given him years ago, "I'm sorry it took me this long to call you back. I just got your message."

"Peter, thank God. Can anyone hear our conversation?" Vladimir asked, thinking he again heard a noise outside the cabin.

"No. Vlad, tell me what's going on? Are you OK?" Peter inquired, his voice heavy with worry.

"Peter, listen closely. I may not have much time," Vladimir answered, his eyes probing the landscape beyond the windows. "There may be three more bombs. I overheard them talking about New York, Tel Aviv, and London."

"Vladimir, where are you? Who said this?" Peter asked, half in shock, the other half taking notes.

"There were six of them. Ashraf, himself, was there." He named the other five. Then, his voice breaking, "Peter, these are the men responsible for what happened in Washington."

The noises outside now sounded like voices, Vladimir thought. "Peter, I think someone's outside. I'll call you back." Then, sensing the tenuousness of his predicament, he added. "I love you, Peter."

PETER SAT STUNNED for a moment, the phone still by his ear. He quickly called the Senate Majority Leader's back line, waking up his secretary.

"Janice, is the senator in?"

"No, who is this?" a woman answered, half asleep.

"It's Peter Hart. Janice, this is urgent. Listen carefully." He told her about Ashraf and the other three bombs.

Just as he was completing the call, he peered out from the RV and saw Enrique crouched by the tire nearest his window, removing what looked like a large pressure gauge from a small, gun-shaped tool.

"Enrique, what are you doing?" he asked.

"Just checking your tires," Enrique responded, flashing his trademark smile. "I know it's late, but I promised Terra."

Peter wasn't sure whether the young man was telling the truth, but it sounded plausible enough, so he let it go. Had he overheard the conversation? he worried.

Fortunately for Peter, he had. It was the only reason Peter was still alive.

Chapter Ten

Friday, May 14th—Los Angeles

RABIA CLAPPED HER hands three times, and the crowd of several hundred came to attention at the mosque. "Salaam, and welcome," she began, placing her two palms together and bowing her head slightly toward the group.

Peter wasn't scheduled to speak until noon, but many from the RV caravan had come early to learn how to dance Sufi style. "The Sufi tradition," Rabia continued, "is an ancient and mystical sect of Islam.

"When you sing, you pray twice," explained Rabia. "And when you sing and dance, you pray thrice." With that she had them form two circles, one within the other, with the people on the inside facing those on the outside.

She grabbed Peter's hand and pulled him toward her. "Now make eye contact with the person directly opposite you," Rabia added, winking at Peter. Then in a commanding voice she declared, "Behold and give the divine."

Peter closed his eyes and took one of his slow, deep breaths. When he opened his eyes, Rabia was looking at him, smiling and radiant. Peter wasn't one to see auras, but a distinct white glow surrounded her body. He was surprised, but strangely relaxed.

Rabia then sang, loudly enough for the group to follow, "I open my eyes to you," cupping her hands over her eyes and then lifting them like butterflies peeling off to play. Peter followed her lead. He so loved looking at her eyes; they were like deep pools of love.

"I open my heart to you," continued Rabia, still singing loudly. This time she placed her hands over her chest and then expanded them outward and to the side. Peter did the same. He was joyously lost now, and willing to follow wherever the dance took him.

"Together we lift our hearts to the sun," sang Rabia sweetly, taking Peter's hands and raising them with hers in a gentle arch over their heads. He flashed back to the day he and Marisa were married, and how her father had walked them out of the small, Midwestern church under a canopy of congregate arms.

Rabia then guided Peter to rotate with her in a tight circle as they continued to hold one another's hands above their heads. Still looking at one another, she concluded the song with "And together we are opening our loving hearts as one." She paused, longer than she usually did at this point in the song, for she seemed as lost in Peter's eyes as he was in hers.

Someone coughed, bringing their songbird leader back to earth. Rabia then instructed everyone to bow to their respective partners.

"OK, everybody," she said loudly, regaining her composure. "Now for the *sema*, the traditional Sufi ecstatic dance of turning."

She asked everyone to spread out. "You've heard the term whirling dervishes?" she asked. "Well, this is where it comes from."

She stretched her arms out from her sides and began to twirl on her right foot, moving her left periodically to keep balance. "As you spin, give yourself to the Great One, Allah, God, Spirit, however it is you experience the Presence."

Peter was struck by her choice of words, especially the Presence. Another sign that their souls were connected, he said to himself, gleaming within at the thought, as he lost himself in the turning.

BEAR HESITATED AS he walked into the mosque. The crowd had grown to 10,000, and it was still two hours before Peter was scheduled to speak.

"Sorry to bother you, doc," he said, tapping Peter on the shoulder in the midst of his turning. "But we got a problem. The cops are estimating that as many as 50,000 could show up today."

Peter cocked his head to the side, unsure if he had heard correctly. "Did you say 50,000?" he asked, his mind grappling to imagine what such a crowd would look like.

Bear nodded. "It's a good thing we've got that park across the way, and the cops are cool about blocking off the street. You OK stumping from the steps outside instead of speaking from inside the mosque?"

"Yeah, no problem," replied Peter, still dazed by the projected size of the crowd. "It's a beautiful day anyway."

"You got that right," responded Bear, giving Peter a thumbs-up. "I'll get Enrique and some of the other volunteers to lay cable across the street so we can run sound out there." Retreating, he added over his shoulder, "This thing's really taking off, doc."

"I know," Peter mumbled, gazing vacantly into space.

Rabia ended the turning and watched Peter walk to the corner of the mosque to pray in the tradition of his mother.

She smiled at how their paths kept crossing. At Reed, now here—even Peter's Islamic roots. She swallowed, trying not to feel the rising anxiety in her chest. But her breathing quickened, as her attraction to Peter broke through her defenses.

It had been ten years since her divorce. Her ex-husband had fought for custody of their thirteen-year-old son, and won. Devastated, she vowed to never love again. She had kept that promise, she realized, until now. How ironic, she laughed: the poet of love and reconciliation with a fortress of stone around her heart.

Construction of those walls had begun earlier, she reflected. She was only four when Israel declared independence in 1948 and was attacked by its Arab neighbors. As Rabia watched Peter pray, the memory of her father being wounded during mid-day prayers surfaced like a dead fish.

She remembered how desolate she felt when they were forced from their farm after the Arabs lost the war. Her dad set up shop in Jerusalem, but died soon after. Her mother insisted it was from a broken heart—that he never got over losing the land that had been theirs for centuries.

A tear rolled down Rabia's cheek as she recalled how bitter she had been as a child, and how her earliest poems were not of love, but of anger. She even joined a militant Islamic organization. Thank God, she reflected, looking at the dome over her head, that a scholarship took her to Columbia in New York, where encounters with Beat poets during the early '60s began her gradual conversion toward peace and reconciliation.

It was still a struggle to trust, both God and man—particularly men, she smiled. But as she continued to watch Peter from a distance, her smile broadened. Perhaps she might learn to love again, rather than just write about it.

PETER FINISHED PRAYING a few seconds before noon and climbed atop a small platform hastily erected on the steps of the mosque. Silently facing a throng of over 50,000, he took the pulse of the moment. Then riding the energy of the crowd like a hawk on an updraft, he closed his eyes and asked Spirit to guide him.

"Relax, trust in me," came the voice from within. "The love you feel, speak from that," God coaxed. "Always speak from that."

Peter's body quieted. His arms were hoisted up by invisible wires, calming the crowd as if cradled by a gentle hand. "Oh God of many nations," he began, his palms open and reaching, "we ask that You guide us as we endeavor to understand and love one another as You love and understand us. May that love bathe the innocent souls of those who perished in Washington, and may it soften our hearts as we wrestle with our anger and grief."

The assembly grew silent, except for an occasional baby crying in the distance. Building on that shared experience, Peter continued: "We are each unique and precious children of God, despite our different languages and faiths. This is the first of what must become, as Einstein called them, our new 'modes of thinking'," Peter asserted, recapping his earlier sermons, "if we are to bring about a day of understanding and prevent another unparalleled catastrophe like May 11th.

"Look at the blades of grass under your feet or the clouds above your head," he asked the gathering, pausing to give them a moment to do so. "No two are exactly alike, yet each are designed by the Creator. We must respect these differences, our differences," he pleaded.

"Our second new mode of thinking, call it a modern-day commandment if you will, is to be humble, remembering always that while God sees the whole truth, we mortals see only pieces of it, and different ones at that. I spoke about this yesterday at City Hall," he reminded them.

"Which leads us to our third commandment," Peter continued, raising his voice with both urgency and confidence. He hesitated to use such a strong word, but God had promised that he would reveal to him ten new commandments, and that it would be Peter's mission to teach them to the world. The press, too, had begun to refer to his speeches as sermons, and his missives as commandments.

"We must listen to each other, graciously," proceeded Peter. "For if we don't have the corner on truth," he reminded them, "and we don't," he whispered, aware on some level of the paradox of what he was saying, "then we must strive to understand rather than convert, to listen respectfully rather than harangue and berate." It was a paradox that would continue to haunt him—being a conduit for God, yet remaining humble and skeptical, remembering that to err was still definitely human.

"Look at the people next to you," Peter urged. "Really look at them." Again he paused, letting the experience sink in, as people shyly looked at one another. "Too many of us believe that we have the corner on truth and that these other folks don't.

"Which is why we must truly listen to one another, to courteously understand, stand under, our different experiences of faith. For when we feel slighted and disrespected, look out. But when we feel listened to and understood, we feel valued, and loved. And you know what?" he laughed, "there's a bonus—we might even learn something."

Peter paused to feel the moment and to reconnect with the Presence. Then sensing it was time to wrap up, he concluded: "Which is why our third commandment must be to genuinely and respectfully listen to one another, to understand more than convert. The future of the world, my friends, literally depends on it."

He ended again with "God bless you, God bless America, and God bless the world's many voices of faith," and as happened the night before at City Hall, the crowd spontaneously sang "God Bless America."

What was different about this afternoon, however, was that rather than meriting only fifteen seconds on CNN, it became the second or third leading story that evening on all the major networks.

HEPPNER, OREGON

PASTOR VERN CAUGHT one of those newscasts. His contained rage, burning like a furious fire in a worn-out furnace, exploded. What really got him rolling was the video of Peter and Rabia performing Satanic dances in a mosque.

"Damn Antichrist!" he screamed, slamming his fist atop the TV in the living room.

His wife startled but kept her distance, cowering in the kitchen. She knew there would be no stopping him now.

Vern stalked upstairs to pack his bags; the house went quiet as a snake. Twenty minutes later, he tramped back down. He stared through her with glazed eyes before stomping out the back door without a word.

Throwing his bag in the cab, he fired up a mud-stained Ford pickup, and sped away.

"I'm coming, Lord," he shouted, gaping at the coal black, thunderous clouds that now rolled down from the mountains. Surely they were a sign.

"Mine eyes have seen the Glory of the coming of the Lord," he sang, dust and gravel spewing out behind him. Vern was in rapture; he loved the part about the terrible, swift sword.

Chapter Eleven

Friday, May 14th—Chicago

"YOU'RE QUITE THE sensation, doc," said the young hotel receptionist, as Peter and Rabia checked in for the evening. "But a show on Saturday?" She lifted her curled eyelashes and shook her head. "Oprah never does that."

"Well, we've never had a week like this either," Peter responded. "Give Oprah credit, though; she's definitely doing her part to help the nation heal."

"And the world," Rabia added, lowering her eyes.

Peter and the receptionist bowed their heads similarly and looked down at the floor. The young woman ended the brief memorial by clicking the keys of her computer with her long glossy nails. She glanced from Peter to Rabia back to Peter again. "Will that be one room or two?" she asked.

Peter fumbled with his wallet. Not wanting to pressure Rabia, he answered two. He felt like kicking himself, however, after glimpsing the disappointment on Rabia's face.

They rode the elevator staring at the door, neither knowing what to say. "Could you check an editorial I've written?" he asked, breaking the stillness. Rabia nodded sheepishly.

His body tingled as they walked down the hall. He felt like a freshman in college, inviting a girl to his room to work on a homework assignment. Wasn't that the line he used back then? And she a former professor of his no less. But he was fifty-six now: Rabia only five years older.

She sat at the desk while he plugged his laptop into the wall. Kneeling, he was immediately drawn to her legs. She saw him, and their eyes met.

He turned to her while on his knees. Without a word, he touched her hand and moved toward her lips. Her body trembled.

Peter held her face in his hands, still no words between them. His fingers stroked her cheeks and then traced her full lips. Rabia's breath quickened, her lips moving toward Peter in anticipation. Tiny beads of sweat appeared on her throat. She slowly bent back her head, allowing Peter to lick the glistening moisture. Rabia rocked gently back and forth, her body limp and steaming.

Sliding his hands under her back and thighs, he lifted her up and carried her the short distance to his bed. Then he knelt down and removed her shoes. He kissed her feet as she lay moaning, and with unhurried love bites, moved up her calves to her thighs. He smelled her as he would a young rose on a summer morning and took delight in every inch of her body.

Rabia arched her back in pleasure and continued to moan softly. She took a deep breath, as her eyes fluttered open.

Then she stopped. Her body straightened. Reaching down, she brought Peter's head up to hers. "I'm sorry, my love. I want to, but I can't. It's still too hard for me to trust that deeply."

He looked into her chestnut eyes. A smile stretched slowly across his face. "Our union doesn't have to be physical, my love." They sat on the bed, legs entwined, surrendering themselves to the penetrating embrace of each other's eyes. There they remained for quite some time. Neither spoke. They didn't need to; their souls coupled in a peacefulness beyond speech.

Their journey into love had opened a universe of light, bathing everything in the room. They laid quietly together and fell asleep, knowing that their world had changed forever.

RABIA WAS AWAKENED just before dawn by the sound of Peter showering. It was the hour of transition, she reflected, preparing to jot down verse as poets do, when a sheet of paper clipped to the lamp caught her attention.

> My Dearest Rabia,
> Below is one of my favorite Rumi poems. I'm sure you'll remember it; I learned it from you. I used to think it was about the Presence, but now I'm not so sure.
> Still learning from you after all these years,
> Peter

When I see your face, the stones start spinning!
You appear; all studying wanders.
I lose my place.
Water turns pearly.
Fire dies down and doesn't destroy.
In your presence I don't want what I thought
I wanted, those three little hanging lamps.
Inside your face the ancient manuscripts
seem like rusty mirrors.

Tears streamed from under her closed eyelids and down her cheeks. She held the letter to her chest, then folded it carefully and placed it in her purse. Drifting into the shower with Peter, they lost themselves in time as lovers do.

REALITY FOUND THEM quickly enough the following morning, although walking onto the set of the *Oprah Winfrey Show* was a bit unreal, even for a network news veteran. The audience appeared somber when Oprah introduced the show, satellite photos of the burnt remains of Washington, D.C., in the background. Rabia's head was bent low as she watched from the side.

"Dr. Hart, I'm at a loss for words," said Oprah, as he took a seat next to hers, "and I'm not usually at such a loss. But after four days, maybe this is just sinking in. An entire city, our capital . . . ." She choked up, and reached across to touch Peter on the knee. "It's too overwhelming."

Peter held her hand and nodded. Her tears reached in and pulled out his. She withdrew her hand, brushed away a few drops from under her eyes, and sat up straight. "Even the psychologist is crying," she laughed through her tears.

He smiled. He understood her anguished giddiness, and sensed the audience did, too, as people giggled nervously in response.

"We did a show yesterday on coping with grief," continued Oprah, "and we could probably talk about it all week, but that's not why you're here today."

Peter nodded again. Cameras moved in.

"I invited you because of your message of hope. You've captivated the country during a most trying time. Tens of thousands have come to hear you speak." She paused, and smiled at Peter. "You're the psychologist," she said. "Why are we so drawn?"

Peter had watched *Oprah* before, but always from the safe harbor of his living room. He had never been in the middle of one of these storms, much less during such a tumultuous time. He reminded himself of his advice to others: forget about the cameras, get in touch with your message, and voice it from the heart.

"If the attack on Washington teaches us anything," he began, looking at Oprah, "it's that our old ways of handling conflict *must* change. We owe it to the victims and their families. We owe it our ourselves. And we owe it to our children. How many more people must we lose? The take-home lesson here is clear: we either change, or perish—period."

Oprah clearly liked what she heard, but challenged him nonetheless. "True enough, but many of us have known this for years. What makes you think you can do something about it now?"

"Because of Washington," he answered. "The horror and sheer scope of this disaster. We know now, truly, that we *have* to do something." He stopped for a moment. "To be honest, I'm not sure we *can;* but I know we have to try."

Oprah looked surprised by his candor, but as a warrior for change herself, she appeared to understand the sentiment. "Indeed," she agreed. Then shifting gears: "Dr. Hart, to date you've laid out what are being called three commandments. Can you share with us the others?"

"I've only just received number four myself," Peter replied. "I can share that one with you, if you'd like."

"Whoa, now," Oprah laughed. "You gotta' tell us about this 'just received' thing first. Do you hear voices? And if so, as a psychologist, how do you explain that?"

Peter felt his stomach churn. He took a breath and centered himself. "Admittedly, this is tricky stuff, especially for a mental health professional," he acknowledged. "But we're all capable of connecting with God—the Great Spirit, Mother Nature, Higher Power, Allah—however it is you experience the divine."

Then, gathering strength and looking at the audience, Peter asked, "How many of you have lost yourselves in a sunset?" He watched as many raised their hands. "It's *that* feeling of connection, of being lost in the awesome beauty of creation. In that moment, you're out of your mind, so to speak."

A woman in front raised her hand, and Oprah decided to go with questions. "Yes, ma'am," she said, pointing to a middle-aged Asian lady in a blue suit.

"Dr. Hart, I personally like what you're saying," the woman remarked. "But what do you say to those fundamentalists who insist that the only way to God is through their particular book, whether it be the Bible, the Koran, or whatever?"

"Excellent question," commented Oprah, turning to Peter.

"We say, and this is important," answered Peter, looking at the woman, "that it's OK to believe as you do. We don't expect you to change your beliefs. Personally, I'd like to see folks open up more, but frankly, it's not for me to tell you how to experience God.

"Your path up the mountain is different from this man's," he continued, pointing to a large guy in a tan blazer, "or mine, for that matter, or Oprah's. That's fine. But let's try to understand each other, and especially not demonize one another for being different."

That got a round of applause. As the noise subsided, Oprah again turned to Peter. "This sounds like it goes to the heart of your new commandments."

"It does, indeed," answered Peter. "And in fact, it's what number four is all about."

"Great," smiled Oprah, turning from Peter to the audience. "And you heard it here first, live, on Oprah," she teased, adding "from the new prophet himself."

Peter smiled demurely. "Well, I don't know about *that*," he laughed, "but the fourth commandment speaks to the importance of repetition. To repeat comes from the Latin, meaning to reach toward, to seek, not once, but periodically."

He looked from Oprah to the audience. "You know how most religions say to pray regularly? Islam, for instance, says to pray five times a day. Or to come to church or temple at least once a week on the Sabbath?" Many in the audience nodded that they understood.

"Well, the fourth commandment asks that we get together with other faiths, once a month, to learn about their spiritual walk, their hopes and dreams. Or if we live in a rural community, say, where we're too far away to get together with different faiths, that we read about them, or these days go on-line." He leaned forward. "Why is this important?" he asked rhetorically, looking around the studio.

"Because what we don't know, we fear. And from that ignorance and fear springs our propensity to demonize others. Once we've done that, made those others less than human—or worse, evil—we're in big trouble. Because then to eradicate them becomes tolerable, even righteous."

He paused, struck by the many different faces in the studio. "Look around you. We are each one in a billion, each on our own unique spiritual journey. The bottom line here is that we truly need to understand and respect our many voices of faith. The stakes are too high to do otherwise."

The audience applauded vigorously. Turning to Oprah, Peter continued, "You asked why so many are drawn to our movement. The answer is here in this audience." He again looked at the crowd.

"The unparalleled catastrophe of May 11th compels us to take action, now. You know that—that's why you're here today, and that's why you applauded just now. We realize that the clock is ticking on the human experiment. We either adapt, change our ways of thinking, or we perish. I hope you'll join us."

The audience rose as it applauded, an unusual show of enthusiasm, even for the *Oprah Winfrey Show.* "He'll be in San Francisco tonight at seven, that's at Pac Bell Park where the Giants play baseball, and then in New York at Central Park tomorrow at three," Oprah said, once the noise subsided. "After that, he's off to London, Paris, and Jerusalem. So if you folks want to join him," she said, looking into one of the cameras, "that's where he'll be."

Peter appreciated the plug. Huge crowds were expected in San Francisco and New York already. Oprah's endorsement guaranteed them.

COLORADO

"MR. PRESIDENT," BEGAN CIA Director Ken Sizemore, snapping open his briefcase. "General," he nodded to Collier, as the three men settled down to business. "Peter Hart's spiritual mumbo-jumbo doesn't make much sense in my opinion, but the information he passed on to the Senate Majority Leader does."

"Good," responded President Norton. "Now we're getting somewhere. What do we know?" he asked eagerly.

"The Russian scientist killed in Iran had indeed been coerced by the Islamic Party of God," continued Sizemore, carefully placing three folders on the small conference table in the middle of the president's makeshift office. "Working closely with Israeli, British, and Russian intelligence we've learned that the bombs headed for New York and London are likely being transported by sea, so hopefully we have some time."

"Excellent," said the president, rubbing his hands together.

"I hate to be the bearer of bad tidings, sir," interrupted Collier, "but roughly six million cargo containers enter U.S. seaports every year."

"He's right, sir," added Sizemore. "We're not out of the woods by a long shot. We still don't know where the terrorists are, and until we do, it's hard to focus our resources."

The president sighed. "Gentlemen, what's your read on when we alert the public? I don't want to panic an entire city, but at some point we may need to." He looked at his watch. "I'll also need to call Prime Minister Kingsmill in London a.s.a.p."

"We probably have a couple of days, sir," reassured General Collier. "We'll have to check with intelligence to know for sure. What's your read on Tel Aviv, Ken?" the general asked, looking at Sizemore.

"Not good, gentlemen. It could blow at any time."

The president ran a worried hand through his thinning gray hair. "If the Israelis are hit, who knows what they'll do. The whole region could go up in flames." His voice trailed off as he gazed absently at the far wall.

Sizemore sat up at the mention of flames. "We must strike first, sir," he counseled, "and destroy every Islamic extremist organization *now,* before it's too late."

Norton stared at Sizemore as if the director of the CIA had suddenly sprouted additional limbs. His first blush of incredulity, however, tapered into a bewildered gape of consideration. "Well, perhaps we could launch pre-emptive strikes," he mused out loud, still staring vacantly across the room. He looked at Collier, who seemed noncommittal. "But Dr. Ryburn has been making considerable progress on the diplomatic front", he continued. "I'd hate to destroy her momentum with moderate Islamic leaders."

They were interrupted by the president's secretary. "General, you have a call—code three."

Collier looked at the president, who pointed to his desk. "Take it on the red line."

While Collier walked to the desk, Sizemore turned to Norton. "Mr. President," he whispered.

Norton looked up.

"About Dr. Ryburn," he continued, hoping his halting tone would entice the president's curiosity.

It did. "Yes," Norton responded, as if to say "what is it?"

"Well, it's come to our attention that during the war in Vietnam, she not only led the Students for a Democratic Society at Harvard, she helped draft their Port Huron Statement and preached violence against the U.S. government." He kept his voice low. He didn't want Collier in on this. "In short, sir, while you were flying missions over Vietnam, she exhorted students to napalm draft boards."

President Norton had felt betrayed by the protests at home, especially while he was a prisoner of war. But that was water long under the bridge, and he respected Ryburn's integrity. "Was she ever arrested for any acts of violence against the United States?" he asked.

"No," Sizemore had to admit. "But she was arrested twice for protesting."

Norton considered the information for a moment, then shrugged his shoulders. "Ken, that stuff happened forty years ago." He shook his head. "Hell, we were all kids back then. Let it go."

Sizemore's gambit not only faltered, it backfired. "In fact," continued the president, "with Joanna's ability on the diplomatic front, let's build on her progress with moderate Islamic leaders. We can use their help tracking down Ashraf."

Collier finished his call and returned to the group. "Sorry, Mr. President." Then realizing that the other two were still looking at him, he added, "Nothing urgent."

"That's OK, Joe. We were just winding up anyway." Norton's eyes were again focused, his voice in command.

"Let's keep a tight lid on the names of the cities," he ordered. "I've got commitments from London and Jerusalem to do the same. We'll continue the full court press for another day or two, and pray to God we don't have to go to plan B."

"What would that be, sir?" asked General Collier.

"Ken's plan to bomb the hell out of them."

Chapter Twelve

Saturday, May 15th—San Francisco

"DAD, YOU WERE great on Oprah," gushed Terra as she rushed to give Peter a hug at the airport. "We were so proud of you!"

"Thanks, sweetie," he responded, surprised to see Enrique with her.

The younger man flashed a saccharine smile as he extended a hand to Peter. "Let me help you with that," Enrique then offered, bending toward Rabia's bag.

They accepted his help, although Peter couldn't shake his uneasiness about Enrique, especially after that strange night when he supposedly had checked Peter's tires during Vladmir's frantic and final call from Iran.

The memory of his cousin reminded Peter that he hadn't told Terra yet about Vlad. "Sweetie, I got some bad news just before we left Chicago," he said, pulling his daughter to the side, while Rabia and Enrique walked ahead. "I got a call from Senator Matthews' office." He folded her hands into his. "Uncle Vlad was murdered."

Terra was stunned, then collapsed onto her father's chest in tears. "Why, daddy? Who?" she asked sobbing. "Are Katerina and little Ivan OK?"

"We don't know," Peter answered, stroking her long hair. "He was murdered by the same terrorists who bombed Washington. They haven't located Katerina and Ivan yet."

Terra was silent for a while as they continued toward the exit. "This mission, dad. We've got to stop the madness," she whispered, squeezing his hand.

"We will, baby," he tried to comfort her, "we will." Then to change the subject as well as inquire about Enrique, he asked, "So how are you and Enrique getting along?"

"Fine, daddy," she answered, cheering a bit. "We're becoming, well, friends," she blushed. "I showed him our house that first night in L.A. Hope you don't mind."

"Not at all," Peter lied, the muscles in the back of his neck popping like Chinese firecrackers. Could Enrique have intercepted Vlad's phone message? he wondered, his palms now sweating as he watched Enrique open a door for Rabia. Perhaps Bear was right about Enrique, Peter reflected, remembering his friend's suspicions about the ethnic origin of the youthful security expert. He vowed to compare notes with Bear as soon as possible.

"My car's this way," said Enrique smiling, as Peter almost bumped into him. Peter had been so preoccupied, he hadn't seen Enrique turn back toward them after helping Rabia through the door. The younger man's voice had startled him; the psychologist tried to cover his fear with polite conversation, hoping Enrique hadn't noticed.

"So where are you headed now that the caravan is dispersing," Peter asked, "what with us flying to New York, Europe, and Asia over the next week or two?"

"Oh, I'm going with you guys. I thought Terra would have told you," Enrique lied, reminding Peter of the villain Iago in Shakespeare's *Othello*. "Made all the arrangements myself; even did the ticketing for you, Terra, Rabia, and Bear."

"That's very kind of you," Peter managed to reply. He couldn't imagine why Bear would let this happen, given his distrust of Enrique. All the more reason to get with Bear quickly.

ENRIQUE GRINNED LIKE a fox in a chicken coup as he drove the entourage to Pac Bell stadium. He had been ordered to infiltrate Peter's inner circle, and he had succeeded. His commander in the United States, a senior officer within the Islamic Party of God and the one in charge of the bombs destined for New York and London, had assigned Enrique to shadow Peter after Vladimir escaped.

Ashraf had suspected that if the Russian scientist would contact anyone, it would be his cousin Peter. Enrique was to find out where Vladimir had fled and relay the information back to Iran through his boss in New York. His mission had been a partial success, for they had killed Vladimir, but not before Peter had passed valuable information on to authorities through the Senate Majority Leader's office.

Enrique's second assignment was to kill Peter when he was no longer useful to the terrorists. Although Peter's message of dialogue was something they despised, for the moment they liked how it softened the West on Islam.

"HERE WE ARE," Enrique said cheerfully, pulling up to a stadium tunnel usually reserved for players. "Good thing the Giants are on the road, huh?" he smiled.

"Yeah, good thing," agreed Peter, shaking Enrique's hand and waving him away from the bags. "That's OK, Enrique. I've got 'em from here," he added.

It wasn't quite five, and although Peter wasn't scheduled to speak until seven, the parking lot was already half full. A head taller than the rest of the crowd, Bear was easy to spot, and Peter quickly made his way toward him.

"We need to talk," Peter said.

"I know," responded Bear, surprising his colleague. "Let's use my place. It's more secure."

Peter was struck by Bear's anxiety. "What's going on?" he asked, as the two friends huddled in the back of Bear's RV.

"That information you gave the Senate Majority Leader was forwarded to the CIA," Bear said, lifting the corner of a nearby window shade to peek outside. "They called twenty minutes ago," he continued, his voice shaking. Peter rarely saw Bear this nervous. "They did background checks on some of us, too—mostly to be thorough, but also because of Rabia. Something about her radical Islamic connections when she was young." He swallowed and scanned the door. "They found something all right, but not on Rabia." Then, looking at his friend, he whispered, "Enrique's a key player within the Islamic Party of God."

"Damn," exclaimed Peter. "We've got to get him away from Terra," he stammered, his eyes wide with alarm. He started to get up, but Bear pulled him back.

"Listen, Peter," he said, grabbing his friend by the shoulders. "I know this is threatening, but we've got to proceed with the utmost caution."

Peter sat back and nodded. He was a thinker and writer; Bear was the warrior. This was Bear's area of expertise, and Peter trusted him.

"We have back-up, but they want us to monitor Enrique," Bear instructed. "Those three bombs Vlad told you about? They're real, Peter, and Enrique is the CIA's best chance to retrieve them."

Peter listened intently, his mind now focused and alert. "But why us? Why don't *they* interrogate him?" he asked.

"They don't want to scare him off," Bear answered, again lifting the shade to inspect outside. "They've positioned a high-tech reconnaissance team nearby, but they think my special forces and intelligence experience during 'Nam could help."

"Who else knows?" Peter asked.

"Only top brass, the three agents in a nearby RV, and you and me."

"What about Terra and Rabia?" Peter questioned. "Do we tell them?"

"The CIA doesn't think it's a good idea," Bear answered. "But screw 'em! They're *your* people. I figure it's your call."

Peter paused for a moment, closed his eyes, and asked for guidance, a process now familiar to Bear. "I'm going to bring Rabia in on this," he said, opening his eyes after thirty seconds or so. "She's smart, intuitive, and speaks Arabic." Softening his voice, he added, "But Terra's too young, and Enrique's too shrewd. He'd sense something was up."

"I agree, doc," Bear responded, deferring to Peter. Then returning to the task ahead, he continued to update his comrade. "I bugged his car, including his laptop and cell phone," he proceeded. "The feds think any contact Enrique makes within the organization will lead us to the bombs."

"I hope they're right," replied Peter, gazing forlornly at the far wall. He sighed and added in a distant voice, "for all our sakes."

AT SEVEN O'CLOCK the stadium and parking lot were overflowing with a hundred thousand people, thanks partly to *Oprah* earlier that morning. It was the largest gathering in Bay Area history.

The energy of the crowd was charged with both hope and sorrow as they joined actress Bette Midler in singing "God Bless America." Peter took a slow breath, thanked the Presence for being with him, and walked from the dugout to the microphone on the pitcher's mound. The audience rose as one and cheered, bringing a lump to his throat. He paused to look at the assembly, soaking in their concerns about the growing violence and the need to end it.

"Ladies and gentlemen, let us pray, each in our own way," he began, his opening repetitious but respectful, "for the souls of those killed in Washington, D.C., their families, and those still struggling with the wounds of this terrible trauma."

After a period of silence, he continued, "But let us also move toward the future with our prayers, so that such tragedies never happen again." Then in a loud voice he challenged, "We can do that by changing what Einstein called 'our modes of thinking'. We *can* light a candle in the darkness," he thundered, "and by doing so shed light throughout the world."

The audience applauded loudly, and although it wasn't yet night, many signaled their support by lighting matches and lighters, the tiny flames uniting to illuminate the stadium in a soft glow.

"To date we have proposed four new modes of thinking, what the media are calling new commandments for a new age," he continued, preparing those in the stadium and the many thousands listening in the parking area for a brief review. "First, to respect the uniqueness of God's many creations—it's OK to be different. Second, to remember that while an all-knowing Creator sees the entire truth, we humble humans see only pieces of it. Third, to listen respectfully so that we can understand one another. And fourth, to learn about the many voices of faith other than our own."

Having updated the crowd, Peter launched into his fifth commandment. It had begun to emerge during the plane ride from Chicago, but had crystallized only moments earlier when he retreated to the dugout to pray for Terra's safety.

"The fifth commandment," he continued, "is to go within before going forth, to seek inner peace before engaging the world." He paused, looked around the stadium, and added, "It's what I did in the dugout before coming out to talk with you.

"Jesus preached 'Seek ye first the Kingdom'," Peter reminded his audience in a soft voice. "Buddha taught something similar when he said 'Look within; be still. Free from fear and attachment, know the sweet joy of the Way.' And the word Islam itself means submission—a Muslim being one who submits to God.

"Such great religions probably don't need research psychologists to back them up," he laughed, "but studies show that when we're angry or afraid, it takes twenty minutes to calm down. Before then the mind is biochemically hijacked.

"Try it," he suggested, "right now. Close your eyes and take three, slow deep breaths." He inhaled into the mic to pace the crowd, suggesting that they imagine breathing in relaxation or Spirit, and breathing out tension and anxiety.

"Feels good, doesn't it?" he asked rhetorically. "The research is clear, and your experience is clear. Cultures around the world and throughout time have prayed and meditated to reconnect with Spirit, God, Yahweh—different words for the same eternal flame—and each discovered that it is the royal road to peace, love, and joy."

He breathed slowly in and out, subconsciously inviting the crowd to join him. As he did, he remembered a story told to him many years earlier by a client. "The young nun goes to the Mother Superior," he began, "and says 'Mother, I am so stressed, what should I do?' Not surprisingly, the Mother Superior says, 'Well, then pray, my child.' But the young nun answers, 'Mother, you don't understand, I don't have time; the Christmas pageant is this Wednesday.' To which the Mother Superior rubs her chin, thinks for a long moment, and responds, 'Well, in that case, pray double.'"

The crowd laughed. Peter nodded his head and smiled. "We've all been there," he chuckled. "But isn't it exactly when we think we don't have time to pray or meditate that we especially need to do so?" he asked, again rhetorically. "For those of you who aren't traditionally religious, by the way, a quiet walk in the park or by the sea can also work wonders.

"The key here," Peter began to wrap up, "is to change our 'modes of thinking', to use Einstein's words, *before* we speak or act out of stress or anger—to pray double. For it's hard to stay angry when you're in the Kingdom, as Jesus would put it, or when you're connected with the Way of things, as Buddha might have it, or after you've submitted *your* will to that of God's, as Muhammad taught."

Peter looked up at a big screen in the far corner of the stadium, which had focused for a moment on a young girl. "That little girl," he proceeded, "and millions of children like her throughout the world—that's why we're here. For if we don't change these modes of thinking, we *will* continue to drift toward unparalleled catastrophes.

"That's what this movement is all about," Peter concluded, his voice rising, "and why this fifth commandment—to go within before going forth—is absolutely crucial."

Touching both hands to his lips, he extended a kiss toward the crowd, holding his arms out as if to enfold the flock in love. "God bless you. God bless America. And God bless the many voices of faith."

While Bette Midler prepared to lead the audience in singing "Let There Be Peace On Earth," Peter searched the evening sky as he stood to the side and wished upon the first emerging star. "Lord," he whispered, like Saint Francis of Assisi had done long before him, "make me an instrument of Thy peace."

"When you pray double," a voice answered, "you already are."

Chapter Thirteen

Sunday, May 16th—New York

PETER AND RABIA WATCHED the morning sun light up New York City as their overnight flight from San Francisco landed at JFK International. Susan Crane, the Unity minister from Manhattan, greeted the small entourage, which also included Bear, Terra, and Enrique.

"I hate to hit you with bad news," the minister said after hugging them, "but you may not have heard. The story broke late last night while you were in the air."

"What story?" responded Peter, cocking his head to the side, his face a mixture of concern and puzzlement.

"There are three more bombs," Reverend Crane announced, handing Peter a copy of the morning's *New York Times*. The group huddled around Peter as they digested the lead story: "Islamic Extremists Threaten More Nuclear Strikes." The subheading read "New York Possible Target."

The only one who didn't have to feign surprise was Terra, who like the rest of the world was now in a state of shock and high alert. Peter, Rabia, and Bear did their best not to look at Enrique, who managed to suppress a grin, albeit not without some effort.

The Islamic Party of God, according to the article, threatened to destroy three more cities unless Palestine was turned over to them to be run as a Muslim society based on the Koran. The extremists didn't specify which cities were targeted, but reliable sources suspected New York, London, and Tel Aviv. The West had until the end of Friday to comply.

It was a quiet ride to the hotel. Bear sat in the back with Peter and Rabia. Terra squeezed in between Reverend Crane, who was driving, and Enrique riding shotgun. Peter almost gagged when Enrique put his arm around Terra.

"They'll track those bastards down," announced Enrique, continuing his charade as the good guy. "Not to worry. We've got the best security in the world." He smiled and gave Terra a squeeze, further nauseating the disgusted father sitting behind him.

Peter rolled down his window as they neared the hotel on Central Park West. "Thanks Enrique," he lied. "It's nice of you to try to cheer us up." If his daughter's life depended on playing games with the little monster, he was going to do his best to protect her.

They headed up to their respective rooms. Peter and Rabia were now officially together. Terra and Enrique, much to Peter's relief, booked separate quarters. Bear chose a room next to Enrique's.

It was eight in the morning, and they were all exhausted. Peter checked in with Bear and then decided to get some sleep. He would need to be well rested before later addressing what was expected to be one of the largest crowds ever to assemble in Central Park. He prayed before drifting off.

Bear positioned himself by the wall adjoining Enrique's room, set up an electronic listening device and other CIA surveillance equipment, and also prayed, but with a more immediate and worldly goal in mind.

AT TWO-THIRTY the entourage crossed the street and entered Central Park. Nearly 200,000 awaited Peter's arrival.

New Yorkers, like the rest of the country, were still in shock, fear, and mourning over the bombing of Washington. After today's news about their city being a potential target, the fear was palpable. Many flashed back to 9/11 and considered leaving. About the only thing stopping them was the Friday deadline; at least they had a few days, but even that was far from certain.

Feeling their anxiety as well as their sadness, Peter meditated along the side of the stage during opening prayers by Cardinal O'Conner, Rabbi Mandell, and Mullah Kolkailah. Besides being staggered by Washington and the possible destruction of three more cities, a central question of faith still troubled him: how could he trust that his inner voice was truly from the Source or Presence, and that he wasn't just another rambling maniac who had gone over the edge?

As a psychologist he knew there was a fine line between a vision and an hallucination. He also knew firsthand how schizophrenics justified the external validity of their voices. Was he crazy, too, he wondered? How would he know? And what about the huge number of believers who weren't insane, but who saw signs or heard promptings from a higher power?

He followed his breath and dove deeper into the Presence. There, paradoxically, we would wait for answers. In the empty space between thoughts, beyond ego, he would catch the whisperings of Infinite Mind.

As he descended into the stillness, he realized that it was ultimately a matter of belief, the proverbial leap of faith. You either believed in the wisdom and validity of your inner voice, or you didn't—but with two caveats.

The first he had spoken about earlier: humility. Because only Infinite Mind knew the whole story, we mortals were always operating from our best working hypotheses. They were still, at the core, only guesses about who or what God or existence was.

The second caveat was that God, as experienced by Peter, was infinitely compassionate, despite such acts of human madness like Washington. The Creator would never counsel violence or hatred; they didn't exist in His kingdom. If you were with God, you were in love.

God was not strident, impatient, intolerant or pompous. He was patient and kind, tolerant like a mother lion with her cubs. If the message was not wrapped in compassion and kindness, it was not from God. This, too, he had touched on earlier, but as he ascended the stage, he realized it was at the heart of what he would talk about today.

He looked at the crowd. He had never seen so many people, and they were all looking at him for guidance and inspiration.

A father with his son on his shoulders reminded Peter of outings with his own dad to Prospect Park in neighboring Brooklyn. How gentle his father had been. He would feed the squirrels and step over colonies of ants if he could. It was his nature, and the brutality he witnessed during World War II, especially liberating one of the Nazi death camps, had reinforced his kind-hearted makeup.

Peter closed his eyes, pictured his dad's compassionate smile, and heard him whisper one of his favorite lines: "Remember what the Chinese say—'Not the fastest horse can catch a word said in anger.'"

Peter glanced at the father and the boy on his shoulders, took a slow breath, and addressed the crowd. "The reason why we are here, especially today, is to explore new ways to handle old conflicts."

The audience was silent. Peter sensed their fear and desperation.

"Time is running short. We're scared, and angry. Einstein's words are more haunting than ever: 'The unleashed power of the atom has changed everything,'" Peter recounted, "'save our modes of thinking, and we thus drift toward unparalleled catastrophes.'"

He paused. "Unparalleled catastrophes, indeed," he repeated, his voice burdened with sorrow. "Can we change these modes of thinking?" he asked. "I wish I knew," he answered sadly. Then, with his voice rising to do battle against the despair and hopelessness, he pleaded, "But we can't know until we try. And this time, we must try with all our hearts, and with all our strength."

The crowd peeked out from behind its malaise and melancholy, and mustered a polite offering of applause.

Peter launched into a summary of the first five commandments, spending considerable time on the last one. It was intimately connected—in fact, it was a precursor, as far as Peter was concerned—to the one he was about to expound on now. "Yesterday in San Francisco we talked about the importance of going within before going forth," he reiterated. "That's because peace begins within. You can't get to peace with an angry heart."

The audience applauded again, this time with a bit more enthusiasm, warming to the subject and the speaker. They knew that what he was saying was true, albeit difficult to pull off in everyday life, especially since Washington.

"I often say to couples, there are two ways to change a relationship," he continued, hoping this turn in direction might distract them from their pain. "Either change how you talk to yourself, or change how you talk to your partner."

These were core principles for Peter, whether the relationship involved individuals, like spouses, or large groups, like nations. "By quieting within, we quiet our self-talk. A key part of that, by the way, is not yielding to the knee-jerk temptation to blame the other guy—who is often the wrong guy, especially at times like this. As the Islamic poet Rumi wrote: 'When something goes wrong, accuse yourself first.'"

A hush settled over the crowd. They were puzzled and unsure where he was taking them.

"This doesn't mean we don't go after the maniacs who bombed Washington," he reassured them. "Not at all. Justice must be done, and the future protected, now more than ever," he thundered, energizing his audience. "But we need to be extremely careful how we talk to the rest of the Islamic world, and they with us. We must stop blaming one another at the drop of a hat.

"Take the swagger and incivility of talk radio," he added. "It's a prime example of how *not* to approach a problem. Whatever happened to 'walk softly and carry a big stick'?"

The audience clapped and yelled this time.

"We need to stop the blame game—both in how we *think* about problems as well as how we *talk* about them. This is where the sixth commandment comes in. Simply put, it asks that we speak our truth humbly, gently, and without rancor.

"The world's religions know this," he proceeded. "Like begets like is a basic spiritual principle. Jesus said, 'As ye sow, so shall ye reap.' Buddhism teaches something similar: karma, the law of cause and effect. There are repercussions for every action, and those for anger are not good," he warned. "One of Buddha's eight paths to enlightenment, for instance, is right speech: avoid harsh and abusive language. The bottom line here is to speak kindly."

Many nodded and applauded. The malaise was lifting. An old lady in a pink sun hat shouted, "Amen, brother," causing Peter to smile.

"Catching harsh or abusive words before they damage a relationship was also crucial for the great Hindu leader, Gandhi," he continued. "He said that effective speech is 'gentle, it never wounds. It must not be the result of anger or malice.' A bottom line for Gandhi was 'the introduction of truth and gentleness in political life.' He believed in the Hindu Veda that says: 'May we never hate one another.'

"So what's this look like in everyday behavior?" Peter asked. "Well, let me give you an example.

"Let's say you're my spouse, and you walk in the door after a nice afternoon with your friends, and this is what I hit you with: 'You're a cold, heartless person, you know that? All you care about is your friends. You don't give a damn about our relationship, do you?'"

He paused. "So how you feeling? Feel like working with me on this?" The crowd laughed, enjoying Peter and the brief moment of levity. "Probably not. You're likely to feel defensive, and for good reason," Peter chuckled. "You were just attacked.

"Now let's change tone. Try this on for size. Same need, different communication: 'I missed you. I guess I'm feeling lonely these days. I'd love to spend some time with you. Think we can get together later this weekend?'

"Are you more likely to give me the 'poor sweet baby' response I'm looking for?" The audience laughed again and murmured yes. "You better believe it," responded Peter, "and here's why. First, I got below my anger. That's pivotal, for underneath anger are often more primary feelings—like loneliness and sadness, for instance. When I talked about *those* feelings, instead of attacking you in anger, you were less likely to get defensive, and more likely to listen to me. Tone, by the way, is ninety percent of it.

"Second, I kept the emphasis on *me,* how *I* was feeling, rather than attack or ridicule *you.* Whether *you're* cold or heartless is up for debate, and probably will be. What's less debatable is that I'm feeling lonely."

The man with the young boy on his shoulders nodded in agreement, causing his son to giggle when his dad's head moved. Peter smiled and stopped to take a sip of water.

"Think about it," he continued. "If you attack or belittle somebody, odds are you won't convince them of anything. In fact, you'll probably just ratchet up the tension and conflict between you. Which is why commandment number six—to speak your truth humbly, gently, and without rancor—is imperative if we want to live together in peace.

"It's the same on the international front. If I hit you with 'You're just a pack of murderers and can't be trusted,' you're less likely to work with me than if I talk about my needs for security or national autonomy.

"Like in the personal example with you and your friends, we still haven't resolved our differences, but we're more likely to keep talking, and a long way from attacking one another."

TOO LONG, CALCULATED Pastor Vern at the far edge of the crowd, as he fondled the barrel of the gun in his pocket. He had traveled to New York to kill Peter and had arrived too late to get close enough for a good shot.

Damn gun laws, he mumbled to himself as he worked his way through the crowd. *Son-of-a-bitch Jew liberals got us by the balls,* continued the inner diatribe. Vern couldn't pack a gun with him on the plane, and it had taken him longer than expected on the street to buy one small enough to sneak past security.

Deceivers and false prophets will come during these last days, he rambled within, slowly closing the gap between him and Peter. *"There will be great distress, unequaled from the beginning of the world until now."* Vern knew his Bible, especially that line by Matthew.

If the burly pastor had needed more evidence that Tribulation was upon him, three additional bombs in the morning news had pushed him over the edge. And judging by the crowd, Peter filled the bill as the Antichrist prophesied in the Bible who would arise during this time.

Tribulation is upon us, he muttered, this time out loud, startling the woman in front of him. She watched him closely while he elbowed past her. As Vern pressed forward, she headed toward the nearest blue uniform.

Vern wasn't sure if the fire coming from his eyes was visible, but he knew that he had blundered by mumbling out loud, and vowed for the greater glory of God to contain himself, as he steadily stalked the Antichrist.

Peter sounded like he was nearing the end of his sermon, and as the power of his words rallied the huge crowd, Vern's fears were further confirmed. *Revelation 13,* he repeated to himself. *The false prophet will look like a lamb but speak like a dragon.*

He checked to make sure the gun was still in his pocket. Vern was uncertain whether Peter was the Antichrist or the false prophet also talked about in the Bible, but he knew he had to be stopped before he destroyed the Church and established a world religion.

Peter finished his speech. Vern could get off a shot, but he was still out of range to guarantee a hit. As he tried to move forward, the crowd joined hands and sang "Let there be peace on earth, and let it begin with me."

My sentiments exactly, you creep, Vern swore under his breath. But with the crowd arm in arm, he couldn't move ahead without raising suspicion. So Vern did something uncharacteristic. Rather than push forward, he dropped to his knees and wept instead.

Those around him thought he was praying, and the cops in front, who were now on high alert, couldn't see him.

While Vern lamented his failed mission, the Biblical prophet Zechariah appeared before him. Pointing a fiery finger toward the heavens, Zechariah reminded the prostrate pastor of what he had prophesied. "The Lord will go forth and fight."

Vern nodded. Renewed confidence blossomed into a smile as Zechariah continued his prophesy about Armageddon and the Second Coming. "In that day His feet will stand on the Mount of Olives," Zechariah quoted himself from the Bible, "which faces Jerusalem on the east."

Vern was in heaven. *Of course, Jerusalem. That is where our Lord will come again, where he was taken from us. And that is where I will kill the Antichrist.* He had researched Peter's schedule on the internet and knew when he would be there.

Wide-eyed and gleaming, Vern slipped away as the crowd dispersed. He would fly to Jerusalem and have two days to plan ahead while Peter stopped in London and Paris.

He smacked his lips at another thought as well. *I will kill this half Jew, half Islamic pig where the Jews killed our Lord Jesus, and where the Islamic devil worshippers defy the will of God.*

A slight drizzle enveloped the sun and cast a magnificent rainbow over the park. Vern smiled. It was a good omen.

ELBURZ MOUNTAINS, IRAN

THERE WERE NO such signs for Leila Hamamra, at least not yet, as she awoke in a torrent of sweat, despite the cool breeze that blew in from the Caspian Sea that evening. She had fallen asleep at her post by Katerina's and Ivan's door.

She drifted outside, wiping the moisture from her forehead. There she gazed at the morning star and heard the siren sliver of moon call to her. She would take her quandary to Allah, she decided. Mother and child were asleep, and the door was padlocked on the outside.

Leila trudged her way up the stony path behind the farmhouse, where she laid her prayer shawl on the grass under an olive tree, and bowed low toward Mecca. "Allah, the most merciful, the most compassionate, please guide me in *your* way," she chanted.

Closing her eyes, she recited a Sura from the Koran, but all she could see were little Ivan's brown curls and mahogany eyes. "How can I kill these people, especially the young one," she cried out loud, "when they are such innocents?"

She glanced up at the horizon as a shooting star fell to earth. *Perhaps this is the sign I've been waiting for,* she reflected, bowing low again—*but what does it mean?* Then she realized that it had fallen over Katerina's and little Ivan's room.

Creeping to the window, she peered in as the moonlight painted an angelic aura on the already cherub face of the sleeping six-year-old.

He reminded her of Azi. Her brother's death had been the final downpour that had triggered the flood of hatred in her heart. He was only seven, she recalled, swallowing a wave of anguish that had risen in her throat, when he was hit by a drunk teenager driving home from the American disco in Riyadh. She bit her upper lip in sad recollection of the Saudi Arabian capital that had been her home before joining the Islamic Party of God.

Her father had blamed America's movies and its loose morals for polluting the young driver's body and soul. But as she lost herself in the ebb and flow of Ivan's breathing, she pondered if perhaps the seeds of her father's fundamentalism and anger had not created her current nightmare.

Watching the tiny boy hug his pillow and sigh, she knew that he and his mother were expendable, now that Vladimir was dead. Ashraf had kept them alive only as an insurance policy, an additional bargaining chip if needed. But their time was drawing near, and it would be given to her to end it.

She hung her head as she returned to her prayer shawl. Gathering up the precious cloth, she slunk back to her room. Her heart needed an answer, but had it grown too callused to hear one?

Chapter Fourteen

Monday, May 17th—The West Bank

THE SUN WAS not yet up as Ahmed Sourani bowed and prayed frantically at the old mosque, the image of two Israeli uniforms on his brother's bed still heavy on his heart. But with three additional bombs in the news, one possibly headed for Tel Aviv, the time for prayer had ended.

"Raji," he said to his older son. "You and Sari wait outside. I need to speak with Mullah."

As the two boys sat close together on the weathered bench outside the mosque, tears rose from beneath Ahmed's eyes like winter rain rising in a creek. He and Khalid once sat like that, and on that very bench. He sighed as he turned and entered a small office.

Mullah Abbas looked up from the Koran. "What can an old man like me do that Allah couldn't?" he chided, for morning prayers had just ended.

"Abu," he called him, for Mullah was like a father to him. "I feel lost in a great storm," he stammered before falling apart. "I need your help."

Mullah Abbas held Ahmed to his chest, then looked steadily into his eyes. "It is written that 'the ocean takes care of each wave till it gets to shore.' We will get you home, my friend."

Ahmed folded his tired body into a chair beside the old man's desk.

"So tell me about this storm of yours," invited Mullah Abbas.

"It's my brother Khalid."

"Ah, the angry one. He hasn't come to prayers since your sister was killed. Is he all right?"

Ahmed hesitated, unsure whether to tell on his brother.

Mullah Abbas waited, then took Ahmed's hands in his. "It's okay. All things are possible with Allah," he reassured him.

So Ahmed told Mullah Abbas about the Israeli uniforms and his fears about his brother.

The old man nodded. "I can see why you are troubled," he answered. "But let us not act alone." With that, the two prayed.

Ahmed found peace for the first time in several days. He now knew what he needed to do. "Abu, will you go with me to the authorities?" he asked.

"Yes, my son. And do not worry. If Khalid is innocent," he encouraged, "Allah, the most merciful, will protect him. But if he plans to murder thousands of innocents," he added, "justice must, and will, be done."

LONDON

PETER AWOKE FROM a late morning nap, propped himself up on an elbow, and watched Rabia as she slept. It was reassuring to have her with him, as well as Bear and Terra, as he began a demanding overseas tour. Enrique, of course, was another story.

Perhaps he needed a distraction, he thought. He lost himself in the simple rise and fall of Rabia's chest as she breathed. He never imagined he would feel this deeply about anyone after Marisa. How ironic, he thought, to be this in love during such a painful and traumatic time.

Her long black hair, streaked with gray, was to him a tangle of delight, hiding behind it the sweet nectar of her arching neck. How he wanted just a taste of her. But the overnight flight from New York had left both of them exhausted, so he let her sleep.

He walked to the window of the old Victorian hotel and peeked through the curtain at the vast green of Hyde Park below. He wasn't scheduled to speak until six. Plenty of time to check on Terra, to meditate, and perhaps—his mind drifted back to the gentle slope of Rabia's neck.

He was surprised to feel her arms around him and her head nuzzle against his back. "I thought I was dreaming just now," he joked, turning to hug her. "Did I wake you?"

"Only my heart, you beautiful man," she laughed, hoping to comfort him and divert his attention, if just for the moment. A revealing silk negligee didn't hurt. Her breasts and neck hooked his desire, while her smile and radiant eyes reeled him in.

He was a fish lost in the savor of the bait. "You know what Rumi says?" he teased her, his face unfurling a huge grin.

"Yes, but tell me anyway. I love to hear your voice."

"'Life freezes if it doesn't get a taste of this almond cake,'" he replied, stroking her hair. His mind was focused now only on her, as his hands, like two lovebirds flying by an unseen map, migrated steadily down her neck.

"Mmm, I like that—the Rumi poem of course," she teased in return. Having pledged their love to one another after their last physical encounter in Chicago, Rabia's trust had deepened. Safe in the harbor of that commitment, she let him slip off her negligee, reveling in the coaxing of his hands. She had been in charge of her life for so long; how luxurious to let go of the controls.

They kept their eyes locked on each other as Peter caressed her face and throat. How she hungered for the fire in his eyes, and how he treasured the love in hers. It was all he had ever wanted, he realized, especially after Marisa died. Love, that was the almond cake. All the rest—the search for fame and meaning and importance—they were just disappointing substitutes, tasteless crackers at best.

He prolonged the enjoyment, teasing her to new heights. They rode each wave with eyes wide open, linked together in love. When they exploded, the room as well as their bodies disappeared. Gleaming eyes were all that existed, portals into vast galaxies of light.

It reminded Peter of his spiritual experience the day of the attack: the same pure love, joy, and peace, he smiled. Tears filled his eyes. "No separation," was all he could say.

His words echoed Rabia's feeling. She nodded, then noticed an aura of light surrounding him. "You're glowing, my love," she said, half bewildered.

"So are you, my sweet," he answered, for her face was surrounded by blue and white light.

Peter knew that despite whatever happened next in this crazy world, he again had found what he had been searching for his entire life, and it was so simple—love. It was everywhere! Why hadn't he realized it?

No matter. He saw it now, and it could save the world. Of that, he was certain.

TWO ROOMS DOWN, Bear was having an epiphany of his own, but on a less spiritual level. He and special agent Neil Hockman had penetrated the files in Enrique's laptop while the unsuspecting terrorist toured London with Terra.

"Bingo," said Bear, a look of satisfaction spreading across his face. "We've got the head of this snake now."

Hockman, one of the FBI's top computer experts,

wasn't so sure. "We've got his boss's e-mail address," he agreed, "but anybody can set up a hotmail account. If he's roaming wireless and borrowing other people's bandwidths, it could take weeks to trace him that way."

"So much for that premature ejaculation of excitement," Bear scoffed, his self-deprecating humor failing to cover his frustration. "We don't have weeks. The whole fucking planet could blow by the end of Friday if these bastards stick to their ultimatum."

Hockman radioed another agent watching the entrance to the hotel. So far no sign of Enrique. He looked at Bear who was pacing the room.

"I think I have an idea," Bear said slowly, his vacant eyes betraying the vagueness of his plan. He cocked his head to the side and stared at the wall in front of him. "Could you send Enrique an e-mail and make it look like it came from his boss?"

"Yeah, we can do that," said the young agent. "Why?"

Bear smiled. "Well, we've read the boss's e-mails, so we know his style. All we do is send a bogus message to Enrique asking him to call, saying it's urgent. When Enrique calls, we track his leader's location and close in on him."

Hockman nodded in agreement at first, but then shook his head in the other direction. "Sounds good, but as soon as the big cheese gets Enrique's call, he'll know their cover's been blown. We'll have to move fast on the other end."

Bear nodded. "True, but he wouldn't dare call his operatives in the field. Besides, even if we don't nail him, I bet we find enough computer and phone records to lead us to the bombs."

"You better hope so," said Hockman. "I'll run it by brass in Colorado. It may be our best bet."

"It may be our only bet," said Bear, "and we don't have much time."

PETER HAD DRAWN huge crowds in the United States, but he didn't know what to expect overseas. His legs trembled as 250,000 Brits, mostly Londoners on their way home from work, poured into Hyde Park.

"Ladies and gentlemen, let us bow our heads in a moment of silence for those lost in Washington," he began.

The audience went quiet as a London fog. Like the day before in New York, the crowd seemed especially anxious. Their city, too, was now a potential target.

"Let us also pray for the safety of this great city. May the power of the Creator protect it, and may our hearts be comforted by His grace."

It was an opportunity not lost on the anxious crowd. The silence deepened, as thousands relaxed their muscles and their breathing.

"You're here this evening because, like me, you want to stop the madness. We can, you know," he tried to assure them. "Why? Because now more than ever in the history of the world, we realize how small our planet is, and how we either pull together, or fall apart."

The audience stirred. They hungered for hope, and found it in Peter's words.

"I have a confession to make," he continued. "When I was a young boy growing up in America, my first hero wasn't George Washington or Abraham Lincoln. It was an English outlaw named Robin Hood."

The crowd murmured its approval.

"Sir Robin of Locksley saw hunger and economic injustice and did something about them," he proceeded. "But what does this have to do with bringing peace to a troubled world? you ask. Everything," he answered, "for we can't expect mothers and fathers to watch their children starve while others eat like kings."

The crowd quieted and grew puzzled. Where was this strange prophet taking them?

"Most of today's madness stems from religious intolerance and misunderstanding," he continued, "but it's no coincidence that the newest threat to world peace comes from an impoverished part of the world. It isn't the mighty Soviet Union anymore, or even Germany and Japan of World War II. It's the underbelly of the world's poor, and they're demanding that we pay attention."

Some in the crowd applauded, although most had expected more spiritual fare than a sermon about food and money. Peter was prepared for the uncertainty, however.

"I'm going to pause for five seconds." He looked at his watch and waited, knowing that the silence would be enormous. "Somewhere in the world a child has just died," he whispered. "From hunger," he shouted. "Six million children die this way every year. Every year," he repeated, his voice gentle but steadfast, like a father at a funeral.

"And the worst part is that we can prevent it—easily. The United Nations says that thirteen billion dollars could meet the basic health and nutrition needs of the world's poorest people for a year. In Europe and the United States alone, we spend more on pet food. Pet food," he repeated, his voice one of disbelief.

"Which is why the seventh commandment is to give to the poor by sharing the world's resources. We can't afford not to, for the world's too small, and the stakes too high. And don't think for a minute that our selfishness won't come back to bite us," he roared.

He paused to quiet his passion. "Take high unemployment in the Arab world, for instance, where a huge percentage of the population is under twenty-five. Crowds of young men with nothing to do, little to look forward to, and no outlet for their testosterone. It's a recipe for disaster." He took a sip of water and looked at the crowd; he wanted the next line to sink in. "For their success is our success, and their frustration soon becomes ours—in New York, London, Tel Aviv, and yes, Washington," he added sadly.

"A few years back," he continued, "a company in the U.S. came out with a shirt that said 'My Way, My World.'

Well, it's time to say 'Our Way, Our World,'" he railed, shaking his fist, "and get on with the business of the brotherhood of man."

Peter's passion now ignited the park. Chants of "Our Way, Our World" floated up from many corners of the crowd.

"What do the world's great religions say about this?" he continued, quieting the massive assembly. "Well, they concur with Sir Robin. Jews, for instance, talk about repairing the world, especially helping the poor. One of Muhammad's first preachings at Mecca agrees: 'He who gives his wealth in charity to purify himself . . . will assuredly be well-pleased.' And Jesus said that 'It is more blessed to give than to receive' and 'Give, and it shall be given unto you.'

"Do you hear them?" Peter challenged. "Giving not only helps the needy, it heals those who give. I remember interviewing for a job years ago at a Florida television station. Before meeting with the news director, I grabbed lunch at McDonald's across the street and bought one for a homeless lady camped outside. To this day, I don't remember the interview," he said, choking up. "But I remember that homeless lady, especially the smile on her dirt-stained face."

That evoked another murmur from the audience, as many nodded their heads in understanding. Peter took a deep breath and wiped his eyes.

"Buddha said that 'If you knew what I do about the power of giving, you would not let one meal go by without taking the opportunity to give.' Well I took the opportunity that lunchtime in Florida, and it was powerful."

Peter waited, again letting the silence work its magic. A light London fog settled on the green, triggering the birds to pick up their chatter. His audience had heard the message. It was time to end.

"Which is why the bottom line today is to take a lesson from old Robin," he said. "Give to the poor and share resources compassionately. God bless you," he said, folding his hands together and bowing slightly at the waist. "And God bless the many voices of faith."

The crowd applauded, vigorously this time, and erupted into a chorus of "God Save the Queen." Somewhere above Sherwood Forest, Peter fantasized, Sir Robin of Locksley bared an impish grin.

Chapter Fifteen

Tuesday, May 18th—Colorado

KEN SIZEMORE CRUSHED a paper coffee cup in his tired hand and lofted it toward the garbage can in the corner of his makeshift office, missing badly. It sailed through the doorway and wobbled to a stop by his secretary's desk.

"Sir, this morning's meeting with the president," she reminded him, stooping to pick up the stray cup. "It's in five minutes."

"Thanks, Beverly," he mumbled. "Patch me through to Peterson before I go, would you please?" he asked, still embarrassed by the errant shot. "I need an update on that FBI gambit with Agent Hockman."

"Sir, did you get any sleep?" she asked, hesitating by the door. "You know, it's a week ago today that Washington was hit. You can't keep going like this, sir."

"I know, Beverly," he reassured her. "I know." He sighed and looked forlornly at a family picture on the far wall, remembering how his cheerleader kid sister whipped the gym into a frenzy when his team won the state basketball championship. He still couldn't believe she was gone. So many lives lost, he reflected bitterly, and for what?

He shook his head as if snapping out of a bad dream, tightened his lips, and returned to the business at hand. "I appreciate your concern, Beverly. Really. But we've got a war to win. This is no time to slow down."

"Understood, sir," she nodded, retreating to the outer office to place the call.

Seconds later a clipped voice snapped over the speakerphone on Sizemore's desk. "Peterson here."

"Fred, we're about to meet with the president," barked Sizemore, the iron door on his emotions again firmly shut. "Any movement yet by that Enrique character?"

"Nada, Ken. But we've got every goddamn Muslim in the country under surveillance. If he calls his boss, we'll be all over him."

"Thanks, Fred. Keep in touch." Sizemore hung up the phone. He glanced briefly again at the picture on the wall, clenched his jaw, and marched down the hall.

Pausing at the entrance to the bustling conference room, Sizemore chose a seat at the opposite end of the table from Joanna Ryburn. All twelve advisors rose as the president entered.

"Please be seated," Norton began. "Joanna, what's the latest on the political turmoil in the Middle East?" His question irritated Sizemore, who thought that military options should trump matters of state at this point. He was about to find out why they didn't.

"Mr. President, Pakistan is in chaos," answered Ryburn. "As you know, although the rest of you might not have heard, President Aziz was assassinated twenty minutes ago." There was an audible gasp from the opposite end of the table; even Sizemore's eyes widened in alarm. "We're still not sure who's in control there."

"We believe, however," added General Collier, "that Pakistan's nuclear capacity is still under the control of General Rashid, Aziz's right hand man—at least for the moment."

"What's the worst case scenario here, Joe?" asked Norton.

"There are three, Mr. President," replied the general. His voice was steady, like a whaling captain in the midst of a nor'easter. "First, if Pakistan's nuclear arsenal falls into the hands of Islamic extremists, they could immediately attack India or Israel. Second, if either of those countries thought that such an attack was likely, they might launch preemptive strikes of their own."

"Either of which," added Ryburn, "besides causing incredible loss of life, could further topple other moderate governments in the area, such as Egypt, Jordon, and Saudi

Arabia. In short, Mr. President, the entire region would go up in flames."

"You said there were three, Joe," interrupted the president.

"Yes, sir. While we might be able to prevent the first two, assuming General Rashid solidifies his grip on power, if Tel Aviv is leveled this Friday, the Israelis would likely go ballistic, sir, in every sense of the word."

"Meaning?" asked the president.

"Meaning, sir," chimed in Sizemore, "that if Israel retaliates, extremists in Pakistan, and elsewhere for that matter, will gain tremendous political support and momentum on the street."

"We could lose Pakistan, sir," echoed Collier.

The table went silent. The president looked around the room, collected himself, and said only one word. "Options?" As a former prisoner of war, he had seen fewer.

"We send troops in immediately to stabilize the situation," answered Sizemore. "Before it's too late," he added. "We're closing in on the three remaining nukes, but if we fail to neutralize the situation in time, we had better be in control of Pakistan before all hell breaks loose on Friday."

"Sir," interrupted Ryburn, looking at the president. "It's not a given that Israel will go nuclear. We've got two days to work with them. But if we send American troops into Pakistan now, it'll play into extremist hands."

She glanced at Collier, then back at the president. "Most Muslims are moderates who were horrified at what happened in Washington. They want stability and peace. Several hundred thousand are expected in Jerusalem tomorrow, for instance, when Peter Hart and the Islamic columnist Rabia talk about reconciliation between the faiths."

"This is no time for faith healers, sir," countered Sizemore, his lips curled in a sneer. "We must act, and act overwhelmingly."

The president looked uncertain, glancing from Sizemore to Ryburn, before turning to his rock, General Collier. "Joe, what do you think?"

"I'm inclined toward limited, covert support for the moment, sir." He maintained his even tone, especially now, sensing his commander's need for direction. "But if we can't get a commitment of restraint from Israel, or Pakistani extremists are about to get their hands on the nukes, then I say we knock 'em out by whatever means necessary."

Norton narrowed his eyes and nodded, as if pleased to see a middle path emerge. "That's what we're going to do," he decided, looking around the room, but mostly at Ryburn, Sizemore, and Collier. "Joe, develop that covert strategy. Ken, check with our people in and around the area. Joanna, you and I are going to get on the horn to key heads of state, especially Israel and Pakistan." Then to the group at large: "We'll meet back here at 0900." With that he rose, his cabinet rising with him.

TEL AVIV

TAWRIYA WATCHED HER husband pace the tiny garage in the heart of Tel Aviv like a large rat in a small cage. Such lingering was not good for Khalid. He was a man of action, not waiting.

"Friday we wash blood with blood," he smirked, wiping hummus sauce from his chin with the back of his left hand.

She nodded, but inwardly, she was worried. "Your friend's garage is too little for a man like you," she replied, massaging his ego, as she crossed the room to give him a hug.

"Allah has been good to me," he grinned. "If the Israelis don't give up Palestine, it is no small comfort, my love, to know that we'll be together in heaven forever."

Tawriya felt her face brighten like the moon reflecting sunlight. She knew he was on to her, and loved how he cherished her anyway. "You are like the Prophet, my spouse," she whispered in his ear—"a messenger from Allah."

He picked her up and put her on the hood of the Israeli jeep. He wanted her, she could tell, but was saving his strength for Friday.

"Does not The Book say 'Fight them', the unbelievers," he railed, "'so that Allah may punish them at your hands, and put them to shame'? We are both messengers from Allah."

She stroked his head. "*Inshallah*," God willing, she replied, losing herself in her husband's eyes.

He peered out the little window that was their only light. Black clouds rolled in from the Mediterranean, further darkening his mood. "'O Prophet, strive hard against the unbelievers and the hypocrites,'" he again quoted the Koran, "'and be firm against them. Their abode is Hell.'"

"*Mashaallah*," Tawriya nodded softly. "Whatever Allah destines."

PARIS

ENRIQUE PULLED TERRA through the lunch hour subway crowd. "Slow down," she pleaded. "The Metro can be fun."

"Yes, yes," he answered. "Only one more." He grabbed her hand and hustled her out a rear door seconds after they entered the front of the car, and just before the doors closed.

"Enrique, stop," she insisted. "You're acting like a madman."

"You're right, my darling," he seemed to capitulate. But that last frantic exit had been his final ruse anyway. He was satisfied now that no one had tailed him.

They walked into the Louvre. The vast art museum had once been a fortress, so it would be easy to lose anyone here, too, he thought. A few minutes later, he announced, "I'm going out for a smoke. I'll be right back." He headed out to call his commander.

She watched him walk away, admiring his tight buttocks and determined stride. She had fallen for him too quickly, she reflected. It was typical of her, she continued to rebuke herself; if only she wasn't so needy. It had something to do with her dad being gone so much when she was a kid—even her desire to be touched by men.

She wasn't looking at paintings anymore. She just stared at the wall, remembering how she had cried outside the door of her dad's study while he packed to leave for another trip. She was only five then, but the next day was supposed to be important: it was her first dance recital. Her mom and grandparents had come, but daddy drove away to shoot another TV series. She bit down on her teeth as she reconstructed the scene. His broadcasting career—and his damn ego—always came first.

Thank God for her therapist, she smiled. After two years of weekly meetings, she had finally figured it out: dad's obsession had triggered hers. The fame of being a network correspondent had filled the hole left by his mother's absence, but in the process of assuaging *his* pain, he had inadvertently dug a hole for *her.*

She looked up at the light coming in through a window and swore an oath: this would be the last time she would fill that void with the love of a man she barely knew.

She smiled as she waited for Enrique to return. Today would be the dawn of a new day. Like the caterpillar who sheds its cocoon and moves on, she was ready. She could feel the wings expanding within her.

Enrique's mission was more immediate, and more pressing: should he risk a cell call to his commander? He had obsessed about it all morning, but his boss's e-mail had sounded too urgent to ignore. He didn't expect any problems, but Terra would be his insurance policy just in case.

"Commander," he said nervously. "I called as soon as I thought it was safe."

"Who is this?" asked the suspicious voice on the other end of the satellite connection.

"It's Enrique," he answered. He stopped breathing. Something was not right.

"Why are you calling me? Is something wrong?" The voice was worried now.

"No, sir. I'm only responding to your email," he replied, sensing something was wrong—with his call.

There was a long pause. "What email, you idiot? You know you're not supposed to call me." His boss was furious, but contained. "You've been compromised. And now, I'm afraid, so am I, and possibly the entire network. Take evasive action immediately. And do not call again."

The phone went dead. So did Enrique's brain. He just stood there, stunned, the phone still pressed to his ear. All around him it was springtime, but Enrique's heart tightened and grew cold as he realized the enormity of his mistake and the dangerous road that now rose before him.

He would try not to kill her, he thought to himself as he walked back into the Louvre, for he enjoyed her innocence. But Terra was his only bargaining chip, now that his cover had been blown. He would do what he had to.

Like a Parisian mime, he modified his face to mimic a young lover. "Darling," he said, finding her not far from where he had left her. "It's such a magnificent day. Let's take a taxi out to Versailles. You'll love the old palace, and the gardens are spectacular."

"Sounds like fun," she answered, studying his face. "It's good to see you back to your old self." He went to kiss her, but she only gave him her cheek.

BOIS DE BOULOGNE, PARIS

PETER LOOKED OUT over the park that had been given to the city by Napoleon III and was as worried as the 300,000 anxious souls he was about to address. In Peter's case, however, his anxiety wasn't only about terrorism. Terra hadn't returned. Thank God she had called to say she'd be late, otherwise—well, he wasn't quite ready to test his faith to that degree.

He extended his hands out to his sides, palms up, and asked the audience to pray with him. A great silence settled over the park. It was a healing time, for Peter and for the crowd.

Despite the shock, sadness and worry of the week, it was still springtime in Paris, the City of Light, and the Eiffel Tower, visible across the Seine, glistened in the slanting rays of a setting sun.

Peter looked down at the speech he had written, and which Rabia had translated into French, and then up to the heavens. "Did not the Lord say 'Thou shalt have no other gods before me?'" he asked them, now warming to the subject. He then repeated it in Arabic, knowing that Muslims were the second largest religious group in France, larger than all the Protestant denominations put together.

"This, one of the original Ten Commandments, must also become one of ours. But what does it mean?" he challenged. "Do you think God intends this only for Jews?" he asked. "Perhaps only Christians," he teased. "And what about Muslims? Or Hindus? Does God mean to exclude Buddhists?" he continued, his tone one of gentle incredulity. Then, raising his voice, he asked, "Or do you believe, as I do, that he is talking to all of us, the many voices of faith?"

The crowd shouted "*Oui*," yes, and chanted "many voices of faith" in French.

"But it is more than this," he quieted them. "Let me tell you about a young prince who wished to be king—not just any king, but a wise and compassionate king. He traveled for many days until he came to the kingdom of a ruler known for his wisdom and compassion. And he asked, 'Oh, great king, how can I become as wise and compassionate as you?'

"The wise king answered: 'I will tell you, but on one condition.'

"'Certainly,' agreed the eager prince.

"'You must spend the entire night balancing this full pail of water upon your head. If you make it till sunrise, I will tell you the secret. But if you spill even one drop from the bucket, you will be put to death immediately.'

"The young prince hesitated, as you might imagine, but agreed, for he was determined to become a wise and compassionate leader. Ultimately, his great focus and concentration prevailed, and the next morning he appeared before the king. 'So tell me, great one, what is the secret to becoming as wise and compassionate a ruler as you?'

"The king answered in a serious voice, but with great love: 'You must hold God above your head, young prince, as carefully and as steadily as you held that pail of water.'"

Peter paused, allowing his message to sink in, as murmurs of acknowledgment floated across the park. "And so I say to you today," he continued, "that our eighth commandment is to put God first—above money, power, hatred, and revenge—to hold God, the Creator, the Presence, above our heads as carefully and as steadily as the prince held that pail of water."

Peter closed his eyes and waded into the stillness. He remembered a Sura from the Koran that his mother sang to him at bedtime. "'By the bright morn, And by the night when all is still,'" Peter recited, the crowd hushed and receptive, "'Thy Lord has not left thee . . . .' That was told to the Prophet Muhammad during the early days of his struggle," Peter told them.

"Jesus said something similar. 'I am leaving you with a gift—peace of mind and heart! And the peace I give isn't fragile like the peace the world gives. So don't be troubled or afraid . . . .'

"God is here. God is now." Peter was lost in rapture now. "It is not God, Higher Power, the Holy Spirit, or Allah who forgets us. It is we who forget Him. The pail of water, remember? For when we do remember, we are at peace, not troubled or afraid. We remember to love, not to hate.

"We put God first not only because it's right, but because it brings us peace. It works," he shouted, feeling more like a cheerleader at a pep rally than the international spiritual leader he had become.

"How do we learn to love God?" he asked. "Your great philosopher, Jean Camus, told us how. 'If you want to love God,' he said, 'begin as a mere apprentice, and the very power of love will lead you on to become a master in the art.'

"So become a master. Put God first. Join us on this spiritual journey." The crowd was roaring now, many shouting "*Oui*" after each exhortation.

"There's a Jewish prayer on Chanukah," Peter continued, quieting them for a moment as he prepared to close, "which says that 'Days pass and years vanish, yet we walk sightless among miracles.' Let us open our eyes," he cried out. "Let us open our hearts." The crowd went wild again; Peter's hope was their hope. "We can do this," he ended. "Together we can do this!"

But even in the midst of ecstasy, Peter silently prayed for protection. "If you are everywhere," he begged within, "please be with my little Terra."

STAMFORD, CONNECTICUT

ENRIQUE'S BOSS, A Saudi sheik and oil trader by the name of Salem Abdallah, had barely escaped when the FBI closed in on his Manhattan office. He had managed to take his laptop and most of his sensitive files with him before fleeing, but a larger computer, fax machine, and other documents still remained.

Like ants scurrying over leftover crumbs, agents worked feverishly to digest what they could, and were now at the door of the sheik's ten acre home on the Long Island Sound in Connecticut.

"FBI. We have a warrant to search the premises," announced an Egyptian born agent in English and Arabic, as a dozen more raced past him. Abdallah's wife, Arin, blinked her eyes in disbelief.

"There must be some mistake," she protested, unaware of her husband's involvement.

"There's no mistake, ma'am," said the agent, slapping two e-mails in her hand. "These are from Ashraf to your husband," he said angrily. "We printed them off his computer in Manhattan."

Arin stared blankly at the papers.

"We believe he knows who's in control of the bombs headed for New York and London and where those bombs are," continued the agent, lowering his voice as if not to scare her. "Any help you could give us, ma'am, could save hundreds of thousands of lives."

Still unable to respond, Arin gazed out the window in shock, repeating "This can not be," over and over like a mantra.

A teenage boy stormed into the room. "These are lies," he screamed, "Zionist lies. My father would never hurt anybody." He looked at his mother in disgust. "Tell them."

She turned to her son, but said nothing, the blank look still on her face.

A younger child, seven-year-old Hakim, came downstairs and raised his hand like a schoolboy. "I know where his quiet place is," he announced in a soft voice.

His older brother shook his head no, but Hakim answered, "These are FBI guys; we watch them on TV. They help people," he smiled.

Hakim lead them to a small room hidden behind a bookcase in the study.

"Thanks, son," said the agent in Arabic, kneeling beside him and draping his FBI jacket around the beaming Hakim. "Allah smiles on you, for today you are a hero and may have saved many innocents."

Chapter Sixteen

Wednesday, May 19th—Jerusalem

PASTOR VERN CHECKED the scope of the rifle and swept a wet tongue over his lower lip. It hadn't been easy buying a gun in Jerusalem, he grunted, especially for a tourist. But he fancied himself a determined man, and as his father had beaten into him when he was a child, there were always avenues for determined men.

One shot to the heart and this false messiah will be on his way to hell, he smiled to himself. He paid the fidgety dealer, stuffed the rifle in a duffel bag, and left through the back door.

Peter would deliver the last of his scheduled sermons tonight and tomorrow at the Western Wall, and this angel of death from Heppner, Oregon, would be ready for him. Vern didn't have a room overlooking the plaza yet, but the inn-keeper assured him that tomorrow he would. Its balcony provided a clear and undisturbed shot. He would bide his time till then.

Meanwhile he toured the city's holy sites and was surprised at how the Old City of Jerusalem so captivated his soul. He wept as he walked the Via Dolorosa, the Path of Sorrows, where Jesus had painfully marched to his crucifixion.

I will avenge your death, Lord, Vern sobbed, his fist raised to the heavens. *And I will prepare for your coming,* he comforted himself between lamentations, nodding his head and grinning like a madman.

THREE BLOCKS SOUTH at the Western Wall, Peter was doing some weeping of his own, for Terra hadn't returned the night before in Paris.

Bear had convinced him to continue on to Jerusalem. It had been a painful decision for Peter, but there was nothing the anxious father could do in France, argued his photographer, and the former Green Beret had promised to remain in Paris to work closely with authorities in their hunt for Enrique.

Peter looked forlornly at the wall and then back at Rabia. "My father believed that the Divine Presence resides eternally over this wall," he said, brushing back tears. "The Roman's may have destroyed the Second Temple," he would say, "but not our people."

Rabia enfolded her arms around him like a mother bird surrounds a chick with her wings. "Your father was a very wise man," she replied.

Peter leaned his head back to look at her and smiled slightly. "And you are a very wise and kind woman." He pecked her gently on the forehead. "A rabbi once said about this wall that 'there are men with hearts of stone and stone with hearts of flesh.'" He touched his fingers to his lips and then pressed his hands against the wall, as if to convey a kiss to the sacred stones.

Then he knelt and prayed, his tears falling on the ancient rock. He marveled at how the sun evaporated their moisture and carried it up to the Divine Presence his father had worshipped so long ago, the same mysterious force Peter prayed to now. He pictured its light surrounding and protecting Terra, a meditation his Unity church congregation practiced back home.

An image of his father came to him, bending in prayer at the old temple in Brooklyn. "'Thou wilt keep him in perfect peace whose mind is stayed on thee.' Do you remember, Peter?" his father asked, taking off his glasses and looking up from the Torah at him.

Peter nodded. How could he forget his dad's favorite quote from Isaiah. He thanked him, took a slow breath, and opened his eyes. Rabia was kneeling beside him. Not many Islamic women would pray at the Western Wall, he chuckled.

She opened her eyes and looked at Peter. "You look peaceful, my love," she commented, gently stroking the side of his head.

"Yeah, I needed this," he sighed. "But now it's your turn, and my mother's," he laughed, realizing the Freudian hay that could be made from such a remark.

They walked up a ramp to the Temple Mount and approached the magnificent blue and golden Dome of the Rock, the sacred place where Muslims believed Muhammad made his Night Journey astride his horse to visit Allah in Heaven.

"My mother was a young woman when she met my father in Cairo," Peter remarked, as he stared in awe at the 45,000 exterior tiles installed during the 16th century. "She had always wanted to come here, but never made it."

Rabia squeezed his hand. "Perhaps you have done it for her."

His gaze veered from the glittering dome to Rabia's diamond eyes. "You're as radiant as that dome," he remarked, shaking his head in wonder. "Mom would have been so pleased with you."

He remembered how fond his mother had been of Marisa, and how Terra had been only a baby when his mother passed away. "All the women in my life have left me," he said in a shaky voice. "I pray Terra doesn't join them."

Rabia led Peter into the Dome, and they prayed quietly. "By the bright morn, And by the night when all is still," he repeated silently in the stillness, "Thy Lord has not left thee." He had shared that Sura from the Koran only the day before in Paris; now it was becoming a mantra.

"I knew my faith would be tested," he said to Rabia, "but I never imagined it would be over this."

Rabia turned to him and swallowed a lump of sadness. "I can't begin to imagine, my love. My son is only two years older."

Peter looked up at the roof of the dome and closed his eyes. But instead of light appearing, his inner landscape turned black. His throat went dry as a familiar scene emerged from the darkness. It was his old nightmare.

A terrified little boy, surrounded by rope-thick strands of spider web, cowered under his blanket in bed. High in the corner of the room grinned the large black spider.

Peter's heart sank; his chest grew queasy. Then it occurred to him: he had not turned this over to God. Why hadn't he asked for help? he wondered. No matter, he would do so now.

God, please help me, he begged, from the core of his being, which had turned to helplessness and fear. Then, as the first glimmers of dawn appear well before sunrise, his soul stirred with thin rays of hope, unleashed by the asking.

A laser beam of light began to cut its way through the center of the web, until the enclosure, like the shell of an egg, cracked in the middle. The large spider descended from his corner to repair the breach, but the laser held him off. The more he tried, the more he was seared by the light, until eventually he was reduced to a small black crisp.

The little boy rose from his bed and smiled. For the first time, he was free to leave. He tiptoed through the illuminated passageway and into the arms of his waiting parents.

Peter opened his eyes and beamed at Rabia. "Faith, not fear," he said. "That's what it's all about." A look of conviction and peace spread across his face. "Faith, and love."

She squeezed his hand, happy to see his spirit return. "I bought something for you while you were checking e-mail at the hotel."

She pulled a small box out of her purse and opened it. Inside was a sterling medallion on a silver chain with key symbols of the world's religions melded together. The back was engraved with the words Many Voices of Faith.

"It's extraordinary," Peter whispered, examining the pendant, his gape of amazement evidence of his sincerity. He lifted the chain over his head and reverently placed it around his neck. "I will keep it close to my heart as a reminder of the Great Protector."

Rabia was surprised at his unusual choice of words, but she was pleased that he felt more protected and secure, as they descended the ramp and started back to the hotel to prepare for the evening's presentation.

CRIMSON RAYS FROM the setting sun illuminated the stage as Peter climbed the makeshift scaffold in front of the Western Wall. The plaza wasn't nearly large enough to accommodate the 400,000 who were expected, so Peter's speech was also being telecast live on big screens at Jaffa Gate and the Mount of Olives.

"As the Jewish writer Elie Wiesel wrote," Peter began, "'I haven't arrived in Jerusalem, I have returned.'" The crowd, mostly locals, roared its approval. To the delight of the Arabs in attendance, Peter added, "Or as the Koran would say, 'We are all returning.'"

Most in attendance were Jewish, but there were also many Muslims, including Ahmed Sourani, his two sons, Mullah Abbas, and a handful of others from their mosque who had made the pilgrimage from Tulkarem.

"And as many of you know," Peter continued, "in the Hebrew language, one doesn't 'go' to Jerusalem, one 'goes up' to Jerusalem." He waited for the applause to die down, letting the silence linger.

"But if we are all 'returning,' and if we are going 'up' rather than just going, where are we going? And to where are we returning?" he asked, as his audience grew quiet and reflective.

"There is a song in Hebrew about this land that sings 'Here is what is good and agreeable; let us sit down together like brothers.' Yet sadly, here like elsewhere in the world, we have not done that. Why is that? More importantly, what can we do to correct that?"

Ahmed thought about his brother Khalid and prayed silently. He understood his brother's anger, but not his actions. Peter's questions were his, Ahmed's, questions. Indeed, he wondered, how can we stop the violence?

"The Prophet Muhammad," Peter continued, "said 'There is no better companion on this way than what you do. Your actions will be your best friend, or if you're cruel and selfish, your actions will be a poisonous snake that lives in your grave.'"

Ahmed looked down at Raji and Sari and patted his sons on their shoulders. Mullah Abbas noticed and smiled approvingly.

"The sun is setting," Peter pointed to the west, "and if it is not to set on humankind, then we must make it set on our cruelty and selfishness. It is time to lay down our swords, my brothers and sisters," Peter pleaded. "It is time to end the violence."

The crowd stirred from its stillness and chanted "No more violence," some in Hebrew, some in Arabic. Raji and Sari joined in loudly. Mullah Abbas glowed.

"Be kind, not violent. Doesn't every faith tell us this?" asked Peter. "The Ten Commandments say thou shalt not kill. Jesus talked about turning the other cheek. And before any reading of the Koran, the first words of the opening prayer are 'In the name of Allah, the Merciful, the Compassionate.'"

Peter again let the silence punctuate his remarks. He took a slow breath and looked around at the crowd. Then on a lighter note, he said, "I had an uncle once describe another uncle as the kind of guy who loved humanity but hated people." The audience laughed.

"But aren't we all a bit like that, some of us more than others?" he challenged. Ahmed searched his conscience. Mullah Abbas nodded.

"It is easy to hate and to react with violence, especially when you've been wronged," Peter whispered. "It is harder to be kind. But that is the bottom line of my message here today," he continued, his voice rising. "Take the higher road. Do the more difficult thing—the right thing. Be kind, not violent."

The crowd was with him now, especially here, where they were so weary of violence. And especially now, with Friday's nuclear deadline looming, and Tel Aviv one of the potential targets.

"As the great Hindu leader Gandhi once said, 'be the change you want to see in the world.' We can end the violence," Peter shouted, his passion whipping through the crowd. "Be the change," he repeated loudly. "Be the change."

Mullah Abbas danced wildly. Ahmed and his sons joined him, as did the rest of their congregation.

But in a darker corner of the plaza, a pastor from Oregon gazed fondly at a hotel balcony directly across from Peter. *I'll be the change, all right,* he said to himself. He looked up at the starless sky and smiled quietly in the shadows.

ELBURZ MOUNTAINS, IRAN

A TRAIL OF dust, like the fuse of a firecracker, sputtered behind the run-down Jeep as it bore in on the deserted farmhouse. Ashraf wasn't expecting any messages from town, at least not yet. He spit in disgust; he didn't like surprises.

He trained his binoculars on the vehicle as it hurtled toward him on the dirt road. It was Nabil, one of his men, and judging by the speed he was driving, Ashraf knew that something was up.

Nabil threw the Jeep into park and hurried to the porch. "Commander," he said, his voice shaking, "Sheik Abdallah's been captured."

Ashraf went silent. He rarely showed emotion when he was thinking, and he was constantly thinking; there was always a Plan B.

He spit again and looked at the dwindling twilight as it slunk from the mountains to the east. The sun had set, he grinned, and darkness was his ally.

He moved quickly now to cut his losses. He said goodbye to his men and ordered them to destroy all documents and laptops before they drove back to town with Nabil. He then told Leila to kill the hostages.

Retreating to the bathroom in the back of the house, he removed the plastic scar from his cheek and the fake patch over his eye. The world had bought his disguise; no one, not even his closest advisers, knew otherwise. He placed the props in his knapsack next to his flight maps.

A small two-seater lay hidden to the east on a flat road that would serve as a runway. He stole out the rear door and into the barn. Mounting his black stallion, he galloped into the dusk-lit hills.

There was still a chance that Tel Aviv would blow, and he wanted to make it to Pakistan by morning.

Ashraf's men tore and burned through the building quickly, then shouted for Leila to join them at the Jeep. She waved them off, Kalashnikov in hand to assure them she meant business.

"This is my final battle," she told them, hoisting the rifle over her head. "Do not worry; they will not capture me alive."

As they sped toward the sunset, she went to the window and gazed through the bars at Katerina and Ivan. They were huddled together on the little one's bed. Katerina was telling him a story, trying to keep him calm midst the chaos.

Leila was glad she had decided not to kill them. Enough blood had been spilled, she concluded, as she slouched to the porch to pray.

She had lost her brother, her soul, and soon her life, she reflected sadly, as she unfurled the beloved prayer shawl her grandmother had woven for her. No matter, she comforted herself; she would be reunited with them soon enough. Soldiers of the Great Satan would see to that.

Kalashnikov by her side, she knelt and chanted her favorite Suras from the Koran. A sniper's bullet ended her torment two hours later.

Chapter Seventeen

Thursday, May 20th—Colorado

"WE HAVE TILL tomorrow night to find and disarm these nukes," began the president, "otherwise—well, there is no otherwise."

A dozen cabinet members and key advisors went silent like schoolchildren who hadn't done their homework. A few turned their heads as an aide scurried into the room and huddled with Sizemore. She handed him a sheet of paper and whispered frantically what was obviously breaking news.

Sizemore swiveled toward the group and cleared his throat. "Mr. President," smiled the director of the CIA, breaking the stillness. "We've found and dismantled the bomb in New York."

Cheers erupted, as the leaders of the free world momentarily let loose like a frat house watching a bowl game.

Then silence again, as President Norton asked the obvious. "And London, Tel Aviv?"

"British authorities are closing in on the London bomb, sir," replied Sizemore, beaming. "That information we garnered at Sheik Abdallah's house in Connecticut led us right to both bombs, sir." More smiles and sighs of relief all around as tight muscles and clenched jaws loosened their grip on a week's worth of tension.

"Congratulations, Ken," said Ryburn, in a spirit of reconciliation.

Sizemore nodded, still beaming, then collecting himself, added, "But we still don't know about Tel Aviv." He again looked at the president. The frat house composed itself. The game wasn't over.

"Why not?" asked Norton.

"The bomb headed for Tel Aviv went by land, sir. The others by container ship. The Sheik, because of his connections here and in Europe, was only responsible for the New York and London nukes, sir."

Sizemore paused and looked down. "And, of course, the D.C. blast," he added. Whatever euphoria had been in the room quickly evaporated. All had lost family or friends in D.C.

Norton was first to regain his composure. "Joanna, what's the situation in Pakistan?"

"Sir, Pakistan has stabilized somewhat during the past twenty-four hours, but we're still facing an explosive Middle East." She glanced at the clock and then back at the president. "If Tel Aviv blows and the Israelis respond against their Arab neighbors, there's no guarantee that extremists couldn't topple General Rashid and retaliate with Pakistani nuclear missiles, potentially dragging India and others into the conflict."

Norton squinted his eyes and rubbed his chin thoughtfully as the rest waited. He looked at General Collier. "Joe, we still have those contingency plans in effect?" he asked.

"Yes, sir," replied Collier. "We're ready when you are."

"We'll wait until evening. If we haven't located the Tel Aviv bomb by then, we'll deploy special forces to shore up Pakistan." Norton shot Ryburn a preemptive look. "And if that triggers an Islamic backlash, so be it. We can't let those nukes fall into terrorist hands."

Ryburn nodded, as Norton rose from the table. "We're not out of the woods yet," he concluded, "but we're getting there."

VERSAILLES, FRANCE

ENRIQUE FINISHED DIGGING the shallow ditch and wiped his brow. The day was warm, but the small forest on the outskirts of town was shady and cool, and most of all secluded.

"I'm sorry, my love" he said, talking to a poorly constructed coffin nearby. "But you'll be safe here, and provided all goes as planned, you'll be free soon."

He could hear her squirm in the thick ropes that he had wrapped around her wrists and ankles. He ignored her as she pleaded with him through the dead cabby's shirt that was stuffed in her mouth. The only sound that surfaced from her pine prison was a muffled whine.

Enrique remembered the shocked look on her face when he shot the cabdriver in the back of the head after asking him to stop by the side of the road. It had all happened so fast, he reflected, and now this drab box, with even darker prospects. Poor girl, he thought, indulging himself in a moment of remorse.

"As soon as I am out of France, I will call the authorities to free you." He hardened his heart as he pushed the coffin into the ditch. "But until then," he laughed menacingly, "you will be my ace in this black hole of yours."

He positioned a stovepipe over several small openings he had drilled through the top of the box so she could breathe, then filled the remainder of the ditch with dirt.

Enrique was preparing to leave when a reflection of light about fifty feet away caught his eye. He dropped to the ground and pulled out the revolver he had purchased on the streets in Paris.

"Show yourselves and drop your weapons," he commanded, "or I'll blow her to hell." He held up his hand and waved what looked like a metallic triggering device.

Agent Hockman stepped out from behind a tree and threw down his gun.

"And the rest of you," ordered Enrique.

Bear remained hidden on the other side of Enrique as Hockman replied, "There's just me."

"If you lie, she's a dead woman," said Enrique, his voice cold and methodical.

"I told you," repeated Hockman, trying not to sound nervous, "it's just me."

"Fine, get over here then."

As Hockman walked toward Enrique, Bear knew he had only one shot, and two lives depended on it. It had been a while since his sniper days in Vietnam, but he had been one of the best, and fifty feet was not far. He waited for the right moment.

Hockman's voice grew bolder as he got closer. "That was quite a ruse you pulled with that explosives threat," he said. "I'm amazed I fell for it. You're sharper than I thought."

Enrique smiled slyly. "Thanks, and this is what you get for falling for it." He was about to pull the trigger, when Bear pulled his. There was a loud pop. Enrique stood stunned for a moment; his eyes widened before going blank as he fell face down on the moist forest floor.

Hockman's sigh was loud enough for Bear to hear. "Not bad, kid," Bear teased the young agent, "for a computer whiz."

They moved quickly and dug Terra out. "Bear," Terra sobbed, hugging her old friend. "I was so scared," she blurted out, her body shaking. "I don't understand. How could he have turned against me?"

"I know, baby doll," he answered, stroking her hair. "He was working for the Islamic Party of God right from the start. I'm sorry."

She stiffened and pulled away to regain her composure. Then, with a small smile, she added, "Daddy always said you were amazing. How did you find me?"

Bear looked at Hockman. "You can thank Agent Hockman for that," he answered. "He's the one who attached a tracking device to your purse." She hugged Hockman, who turned red.

Terra stared at Enrique's body. "I'll be OK," she sniffled, wiping her nose and tightening her jaw like a fist.

Bear walked over to Enrique's corpse and pushed it over with his boot. "If a bad guy falls in the forest," he joked darkly, peering into Enrique's empty eyes, "and only we hear it, is he really dead?"

Bear looked grimly at Terra and answered his own question. "Not until your father hears it." He snapped open his cell phone and gently placed it in her hand.

TEL AVIV

"TOMORROW WE JOIN the Prophet in heaven," said Khalid, checking the settings on the bomb, while Tawriya prepared their final supper.

"But before then, we must eat," she reminded him. "Come, supper is ready."

He crossed the garage which had been their home for nearly a week and kissed her tenderly on the cheek. "Someday our little ones will understand why we were martyrs," he said, mostly to assuage her guilt about leaving their two children.

In a van parked down the street, an agent from the Mossad, the Israeli secret service, spit in disgust as he monitored the conversation, but smiled as he listened nonetheless. "They are sitting down to eat," he radioed his commander, Shlomo Eliezer, a balding man in his early forties, who was positioned with nine of his best men near the small shed.

The Mossad had received the information Khalid's brother, Ahmed, and Mullah Abbas had given to local authorities, but it had taken the agency a few days to track down the location. They had proceeded cautiously, not to alert Khalid.

"Launch project Ha Tikva," Shlomo whispered into a small microphone attached to his helmet.

He and his men had been in position for forty-five minutes, waiting for the right moment, when Khalid would be furthest from the bomb and in conversation with his wife. Khalid would be less likely to hear them as they crept the final few yards to the door.

Shlomo crouched under the garage's only window and carefully raised a small mirror. Rotating it slowly, he scanned the room.

"On my count," he whispered into the mic. "One, two, three." Suddenly the room exploded, as agents stormed through the door, Uzis blazing.

Tawriya was shot instantly, a cup of tea still to her lips. Khalid dove to the floor but was killed within seconds.

The madness was over, at least for the present.

JERUSALEM

THE CROWD WAS jubilant as Peter climbed the stage again at the Western Wall for his final scheduled appearance. The world had learned only hours before about the dismantling of the bombs in New York and London, and now radios and loudspeakers were joyously announcing the end of the terrorist threat to Tel Aviv.

"Today we say Shalom, Salaam, Peace," Peter shouted, "and really mean it." The crowd roared back in agreement, thousands chanting "Shalom, Salaam, Peace," lost in the exaltation of the moment.

"The sun may be setting," he added, referring to the twilight as it painted the plaza with its brush of pink and red, "but it feels more like a time described by the poet William Blake, when the morning star rose and all the children of God shouted for joy. This is such a time," he yelled gleefully. "This is such a time."

Ahmed, his two sons, and Mullah Abbas danced wildly, like the day before, but this time everyone skipped and hopped about. Peter's following had continued to grow;

500,000 attended today at several locations in Jerusalem, while the world's major networks beamed Peter's gathering live to tens of millions of viewers on every continent.

Perelli lit a cigar while he looked on in New York. Even his dour boss Duncan high-fived it with producer Lucy Chang, as Peter's gathering in the Old City of Jerusalem, home to thirty-five hundred years of religious history, again became a focal point for world celebration.

From the safety of a hospital room in Germany, little Ivan watched from his mother's lap as they rested. Katerina hadn't told him about his father yet. She smiled sadly as she listened to Peter on TV.

"During the Middle Ages," Peter continued, "maps called Jerusalem 'the naval of the world.' It certainly is today," he reminded the partisan crowd in an upbeat voice, much to their delight.

He waited for the gaiety to subside. "But back to Blake's morning star," he proceeded, his tone more serious. "Because it heralds the coming of a new dawn, it is a time of hope," he lectured. The crowd sensed a warning in his voice, however. "But this crack between the worlds, when the light of a new day has not yet blessed the horizon, is a time of danger as well."

Mullah Abbas nodded thoughtfully. Perelli reflected between puffs. Even Sizemore listened in Colorado, suspending his usual scorn for the moment. The world waited. They knew that these were dangerous times still, and they longed for an emerging dawn of lasting peace. Peter's new commandments had given them hope and direction. Perhaps this last one would show them the way.

"Somewhere in India an old man is dying," continued Peter. "The wind will lift up his last breath as it leaves his mouth, millions of molecules of carbon dioxide. Several hundred will make it to North America, where a tree will convert them to oxygen. A few will rise into the sky and travel across the Atlantic to Europe. One may make it back to India, to become part of a newborn's first breath."

The crowd grew quiet, imagining the journey, wondering where Peter was taking them. Ahmed thought about his brother's last desperate breath and offered a silent prayer. Rabia closed her eyes, tilted her head back, and exhaled toward the heavens.

"For on the deepest of levels," Peter whispered, his voice tender, almost tearful, "we are all connected." He paused and looked around. He felt the connection, but did they? And more importantly, could he help them feel it?

"Do not most religions, in one way or another, say to love thy neighbor as thyself?" he asked, his voice rising, his body urgent. "It's because we *are* one another."

He paused to let the silence work its magic. "This love, it can not be thought. It's way beyond that. Like anything real, from a sunrise to a full moon, it has to be experienced."

Mullah Abbas nodded. He knew. Sizemore, Perelli, even Duncan—on some unseen level, they all knew.

"Will we be able to love one another enough, despite our differences?" He let the question linger in the twilight.

"I don't know," he admitted softly. "I really don't." Those listening stretched their ears and their awareness, sensing survival depended on the answer.

"I do know that we must try—truly try. In our homes, in our schools, in our prayers, and most of all, in our hearts. For the bottom line is love. We either achieve it, or we perish as a species."

There was no applause, only serious silence, like when friends or family witness the passing of a loved one. There isn't much to say at those moments; their overwhelming truth quiets all thought.

"We dodged three bullets today," Peter continued. "Big ones. But make no mistake about it," he warned, shaking his right hand, its index finger pointed upward, "more bullets are just around the corner. We must learn to love one another."

He shouted now. It was all he had left. "We must learn to love one another," he repeated, and yet again. The crowd heard his desperation and screamed for all they were worth, as if to give birth to love through their clamor.

"Will we be able to do it?" he asked, as the noise subsided. "Perhaps the writer Henry Miller had the answer. 'Let us do our best,' he said, 'even if it gets us nowhere.'" Peter nodded several times as he looked around the audience. "So let us try," he continued. "And let us begin today."

A giant unlit torch was wheeled into the plaza. The bronze statue of many overlapping hands stood fifteen feet high, the height of Peter's platform.

"We are all sparks from the same flame," he said, as he was handed a flaming torch with which to light the large one. Two men and a woman in running attire joined him on stage. "These Olympic runners, with your help," he added, looking straight to camera, "will carry the flame to every corner of the world." Phone numbers appearing at the bottom of television screens around the globe were flooded with volunteers eager to participate.

"With your help, we can do this," he said, his eyes determined like falcons. "We can bring the world together in love."

YEAH, THE FALSE love of a false prophet, sneered Pastor Vern, caressing his new rifle and fondling the trigger.

He had bided his time just inside the hotel balcony opposite Peter's platform, waiting for God's signal. And now he had seen it. *The fire of hell,* he mumbled, snickering at Peter's flame, which had grown brighter in the dwindling sunlight.

Steady my hand, Lord, he prayed. *Make my shot true, in honor of your eternal truth, which shall not be debased by the Antichrist.*

He took a delayed breath and recited the Lord's Prayer while Peter approached the giant torch. The world moved in slow motion for the pastor, as a lone bead of sweat ran down his forehead. He squinted through the site, aiming at Peter's heart.

Vern watched as Peter lifted his torch, the Antichrist now only a step away from completing his blasphemous mission.

The plaza grew quiet. Pastor Vern's finger squeezed the trigger. Suddenly a resounding crack echoed off the Western Wall, knocking Peter to the floor of the scaffold, the glowing torch falling beside him.

Vern looked on as Israeli police swarmed the stage like soldier ants protecting a new queen. One of them pointed to his balcony, as the crowd panicked. Mothers screamed and cradled their children. Thousands began to push their way to safety.

In the midst of the chaos, the mayor of Jerusalem along with a leading Islamic cleric stepped to the mic and did something unexpected: they sang.

The masses below seemed as confused as Vern. It was the Hebrew song Peter referred to the day earlier: "Here is what is good and agreeable, let us sit down together like brothers." The crowd slowed its retreat and gradually joined in, each round growing louder and louder.

That didn't matter to Vern, though. *The Antichrist is dead, praise God,* he mumbled. That was the important thing.

He aimed his rifle at the door as police charged up the steps to his room. *Suicide by Jewish cops,* Vern scoffed, *how ironic.* But Vern was with God, he assured himself, and God would take care of him. He closed his eyes, and prepared to enter the gates of heaven.

Peter did as well as he torpedoed through a long, curving tunnel of light. He had read about such journeys, which contributed to his odd sense of calm.

The karmic umbilical cord dropped him by the side of a wide river. Someone waved to him from the other side. It was Marisa, who yelled with great sadness as he entered the water, "You must go back, Peter. It is not your time, my love."

She floated across and tenderly embraced him before he was pulled, as if by strong magnets, back through the umbilical cord of light. Loving arms surrounded him during his return trip, the spark once again returning to his body.

As he neared his arrival, he heard another voice pleading, "Come back, Peter. It is not your time, my love." He opened his eyes, and there was Rabia, tears in hers, a smile wider than the Nile. "Thank God," was all she sobbed, pulling his wounded body close to hers.

A young medic ripped open Peter's bloodstained shirt. Rabia's medallion had been shot clear through. "Absolutely amazing," said the medic, examining Peter's injury. "That bullet should have killed you," he added, fingering the pendant. "You're a lucky man."

"I am," Peter whispered faintly, looking at Rabia, as he gingerly lifted the dripping medallion to his face. The first three words of the inscription Many Voices of Faith were shattered; only the word Faith remained.

His body was tired, but his soul had other plans. Leaning on the mayor of Jerusalem and the Islamic cleric, Peter staggered to his feet, firing up the anxious crowd and the worried millions who were watching on television.

"Pick up the torch, Peter," spoke the still small voice. "Remember, I will guide you."

Waving off his helpers, he pressed a bandage to his wound with his left hand. Then, like a mother finding strength to lift a car off her infant, Peter picked up the still burning torch with his right. The crowd roared a tidal wave of support as he haltingly lurched toward the giant bronze statue.

An Islamic teenager in Indonesia bit his lip as he watched intently on a neighbor's TV. A young Hindu mother in New Delhi clutched her baby and prayed. A Christian grandmother in Dallas put down her knitting. The world held its collective breath and waited.

Peter hoisted up his torch and ignited the waiting bronze one. "We are many voices of faith," he said, as a large flame gave birth to the hopes of millions. "And we are coming together in love."

Epilogue

May 11th—One Year Later

WASHINGTON WAS EMPTY and quiet; only the weeds had returned. The capital had been permanently evacuated due to high levels of radioactivity, much of which would last for centuries.

From Virginia to the Allegheny Mountains a hundred miles to the west, where winds had dropped their deadly cargo of radiation, babies had been born with gross abnormalities, and farm animals without heads or eyes.

President Norton, from a new White House in Philadelphia, continued his calling by rallying the United Nations to rein in weapons of mass destruction, while building bridges of understanding between the West and the Islamic world.

On this National Day of Mourning, he quoted a line by the poet Mary Oliver, which Peter had shared with him:

"One day you finally knew what you had to do, and began."
He had not rested in that pursuit.

NINETEEN-YEAR-OLD JOSHUA BRENNAN, Vern's estranged son who had grown up with little memory of his father, spent the day listening to leaders of different faiths at a large stadium in Los Angeles.

Joshua's mother, Vern's first wife, had raised Joshua as a Catholic, and their church, like millions of others throughout the world, had adopted Peter's New Commandments, one of which was to meet monthly with members of other religions.

Terra Hart also addressed the crowd. Her quest to move beyond anger to forgiveness spoke to Joshua personally, although he barely remembered his father's abuse of his mother.

Joshua's mom never told him about Vern's death in Jerusalem. Joshua knew only that he wanted to rid the world of violence and help Peter promote dialogue between the many voices of faith. To that end he pledged his young life.

THOUSANDS CHEERED PETER as he climbed the platform once again at the Western Wall.

Ahmed's family and half his mosque had made the pilgrimage from their small town in the West Bank. Although Mullah Abbas had died two months earlier, his spirit was very much with them as they danced and prayed in the plaza.

Rabia joined Peter on the platform and addressed the crowd in Arabic, speaking fiercely about risk and the courage to love. She and Peter had become a team, traveling the globe together, teaching Peter's New Commandments to whoever would listen.

Peter finally resigned as a correspondent, something Bear and Perelli didn't think he could do. And although he was still the center of attention, he no longer needed it. Faith had replaced fear; Spirit had dethroned ego. Like a leaf in autumn, he had let go and moved on. And although vast regions of violence still remained, he was shining a light in the darkness.

Postscript

To connect with others who are practicing The New Commandments, go to **www.newcommandments.com**. Below is a summary of them.

THE NEW COMMANDMENTS

1. RESPECT THE UNIQUENESS OF GOD'S MANY CREATIONS. We are each a unique and precious child of the universe, one of many voices of faith. Respect those differences, and one another.

2. REMEMBER THAT WHILE GOD SEES THE WHOLE TRUTH, WE HUMANS SEE ONLY A PORTION OF IT. No one sees the whole picture; we each have different points of view. Therefore we need to be humble.

3. LISTEN RESPECTFULLY TO UNDERSTAND ONE ANOTHER. So we must listen to each other, and respectfully strive to under-stand, rather than convert, as God understands us.

4. LEARN ABOUT OTHER VOICES OF FAITH. At least once a month, learn about a different faith other than your own.

5. GO WITHIN BEFORE GOING FORTH: SEEK INNER PEACE. Peace begins within. Pray or meditate double when stressed. Sit with pain or anger and surrender it up.

6. SPEAK YOUR TRUTH HUMBLY, GENTLY AND WITHOUT RANCOR. The Chinese say: "Not the fastest horse can catch a word said in anger." Remember to share humbly and without accusation.

7. GIVE TO THE POOR AND SHARE RESOURCES GENEROUSLY. Let us move from My Way, My World, to Our Way, Our World. We are all God's children, so give generously.

8. LIVE YOUR LIFE AS A SPIRITUAL JOURNEY: PUT GOD FIRST. "No other Gods before me" includes money, fame, relationships, and ego. Life is also happier when Spirit comes first.

9. BE KIND, NOT VIOLENT. Thou shalt not kill, remember? Make a commitment to live non-violently.

10. LOVE ONE ANOTHER. The bottom line: be compassionate and act with loving kindness. Remember, too, that what goes around, comes around.

Individual or Group Reading Guide

THE NEW COMMANDMENTS

ABOUT THE BOOK

AFTER THE VIOLENCE of September 11th, many of us felt righteously angry. We certainly were entitled. After all, we were ruthlessly attacked, and for no apparent reason.

But now what? How do we respond? Indeed, how might the world prevent such senseless acts of violence?

At the heart of *The New Commandments* is Einstein's warning that "The unleashed power of the atom has changed everything save our modes of thinking, and we thus drift toward unparalleled catastrophes."

What makes us uneasy about this story is that the fictitious destruction of Washington, D.C., is not beyond the realm of possibility. Like a frightened animal, we smell the potential for such madness just around the corner.

Peter's journey challenges us to answer the question: can we change these modes of thinking—before it's too late? It's a discussion worth exploring.

Questions for Discussion

1) The first of The New Commandments is about respecting the uniqueness of God's many creations. As a nation, do we appreciate and respect the unique gifts of such different religions as Islam, for example? On an individual basis, do we respect our own uniqueness as well as that of others? What might be one step we can take to become more respect-full?

2) The second New Commandment reminds us that while God sees the whole truth, we humans see only pieces of it—and different ones at that. It encourages us, therefore, to approach our differences humbly. Do we do that as a country? How about on talk radio? Closer to home, do we do that personally, especially with our partners, children, or parents?

3) Commandment number three urges us to listen respectfully to one another's points of view. Do we do this nationally with other countries? When we stop listening as individuals, do we mentally prepare rebuttals while the other person is talking? How do others respond when we do that?

4) Do we spend any time as a predominantly Christian culture learning about other voices of faith? Or do we believe that this fourth Commandment is too risky—perhaps opening us up to darkness or evil? To what degree can we stand

in our own truth while genuinely learning how others experience theirs? How important is this for world peace?

5) When we're tense, angry or hurt, do we take a few minutes to calm down before engaging with others? Do our leaders in politics, sports and the media encourage that? What happens when we act impulsively? How important is this fifth Commandment in your personal relationships?

6) As a nation, are we too quick to blame and attack others? Do we feel entitled to our rage? How about on the highway? When we accuse others in anger, how do they usually respond? How important is this sixth Commandment—to speak our truth humbly, gently, and without rancor— both culturally and personally?

7) Are we a generous people? How do we balance that with our belief in capitalism? To what degree should we help the poor and abused, especially children? Do we think of taxes as a form of tyranny, or as tithing to the larger community? How do we feel on a personal level when we help someone in need? Practicing the seventh Commandment may bring us more happiness than we might expect.

8) As a society, do we put God (or doing the right thing) first? Above money? Status? Relationships? Ego? Do we practice this Commandment personally? What usually stops us? And what small steps can we take to change that?

9) Are we a kind society? If not, why? More importantly, how can we become more compassionate? Do we personally practice random acts of kindness? Would we be happier if we did? If we put this ninth Commandment to the test—by offering a helping hand to an older person at the grocery, or a compliment to someone at home or work—how might that affect us in return?

10) The world's great religions talk about love, but how loving are we as a nation? Do we love others personally, or are we irritable, impatient and angry instead? If it's true that we get what we give, then perhaps this tenth Commandment can help us become happier. How can we each express (and thereby receive) more love in our personal lives?

11) When are other points of view too evil or wrong to listen to? How likely is this to happen with friends or family? Are governments and cultures any more likely to be evil, therefore justifying us in not dialoguing with them? Is it worth the risk to negotiate with a questionable country? Is it worth the risk not to?

12) In the New Commandments, Peter was uncertain at times whether his "voices" were from a Higher Power, or whether he was going crazy. How can we tell when messages are divinely inspired? Peter relied on humility and love as filters. Are there others?